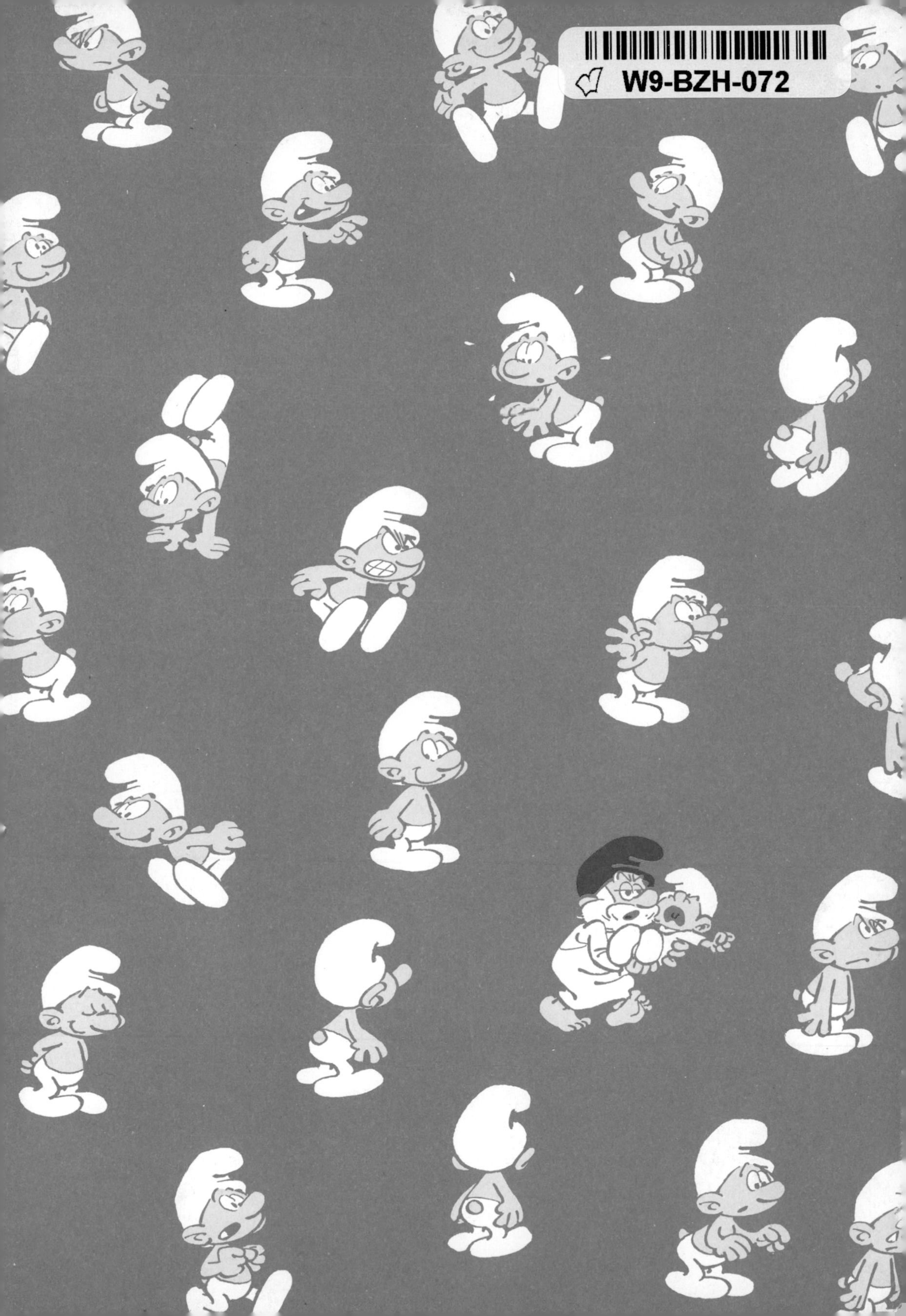

THE BABY SMURF

Peyo

THE BABY SMURF

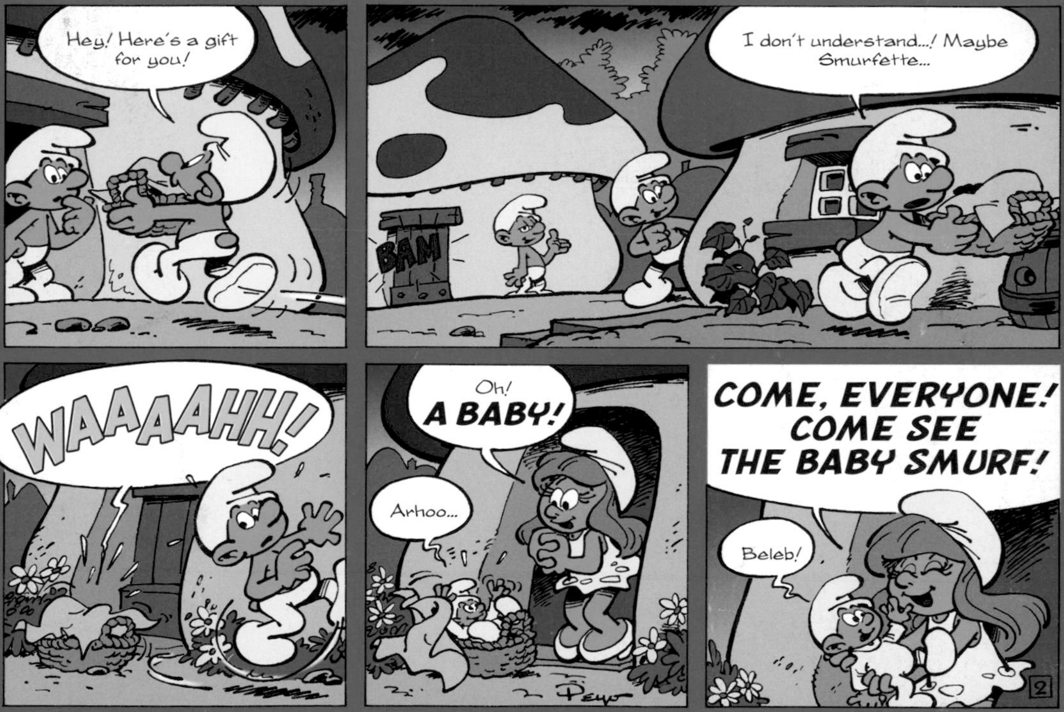
Hey! Here's a gift for you!
BAM
I don't understand...! Maybe Smurfette...
WAAAAAHH!
Oh! A BABY!
Arhoo...
COME, EVERYONE! COME SEE THE BABY SMURF!
Beleb!
2

A SMURFS GRAPHIC NOVEL BY PEYO

PAPERCUTZ™
NEW YORK

SMURFS GRAPHIC NOVELS AVAILABLE FROM PAPERCUTZ™

PURPLE SMURFS
THE SMURFS AND THE MAGIC FLUTE
THE SMURF KING
THE SMURFETTE
THE SMURFS AND THE EGG
THE SMURFS AND THE HOWLIBIRD
THE ASTRO SMURF
THE SMURF APPRENTICE
GARGAMEL AND THE SMURFS
THE RETURN OF THE SMURFETTE
THE SMURF OLYMPICS
SMURF VS. SMURF
SMURF SOUP
THE BABY SMURF

1. THE PURPLE SMURFS
2. THE SMURFS AND THE MAGIC FLUTE
3. THE SMURF KING
4. THE SMURFETTE
5. THE SMURFS AND THE EGG
6. THE SMURFS AND THE HOWLIBIRD
7. THE ASTROSMURF
8. THE SMURF APPRENTICE
9. GARGAMEL AND THE SMURFS
10. THE RETURN OF THE SMURFETTE
11. THE SMURF OLYMPICS
12. SMURF VS. SMURF
13. SMURF SOUP
14. THE BABY SMURF

COMING SOON:

THE SMURFLINGS

15. **THE SMURFLINGS**

THE SMURFS graphic novels are available in paperback for $5.99 each and in hardcover for $10.99 each at booksellers everywhere. You can also order online at www.papercutz.com. Or call 1-800-886-1223, Monday through Fridays, 9 – 5 EST. MC, Visa, and AmEx accepted. To order by mail, please add $4.00 for postage and handling for first book ordered, $1.00 for each additional book and make check payable to NBM Publishing. Send to: Papercutz, 160 Broadway, Suite 700, East Wing, New York, NY 10038.

THE SMURFS graphic novels are also available digitally wherever e-books are sold.

WWW.PAPERCUTZ.COM

THE BABY SMURF

"The Baby Smurf"
BY PEYO

"A Smurfing Party"
BY PEYO

"The Weather-Smurfing Machine"
BY PEYO WITH GOS

"The Red Taxis"
A BENNY BREAKIRON PREVIEW
BY PEYO (WITH BACKGROUNDS BY WILL)

Joe Johnson, *SMURFLATIONS*
Adam Grano, *SMURFIC DESIGN*
Janice Chiang, *LETTERING SMURFETTE*
Matt. Murray, *SMURF CONSULTANT*
Michael Petranek, *ASSOCIATE SMURF*
Jim Salicrup, *SMURF-IN-CHIEF*

PAPERBACK EDITION ISBN: 978-1-59707-381-3
HARDCOVER EDITION ISBN: 978-1-59707-382-0

PRINTED IN CHINA FEBRUARY 2013 BY WKT CO. LTD.
3/F PHASE I LEADER INDUSTRIAL CENTRE
188 TEXACO ROAD, TSEUN WAN, N.T., HONG KONG

DISTRIBUTED BY MACMILLAN
FIRST PAPERCUTZ PRINTING

THE SMURF BABY

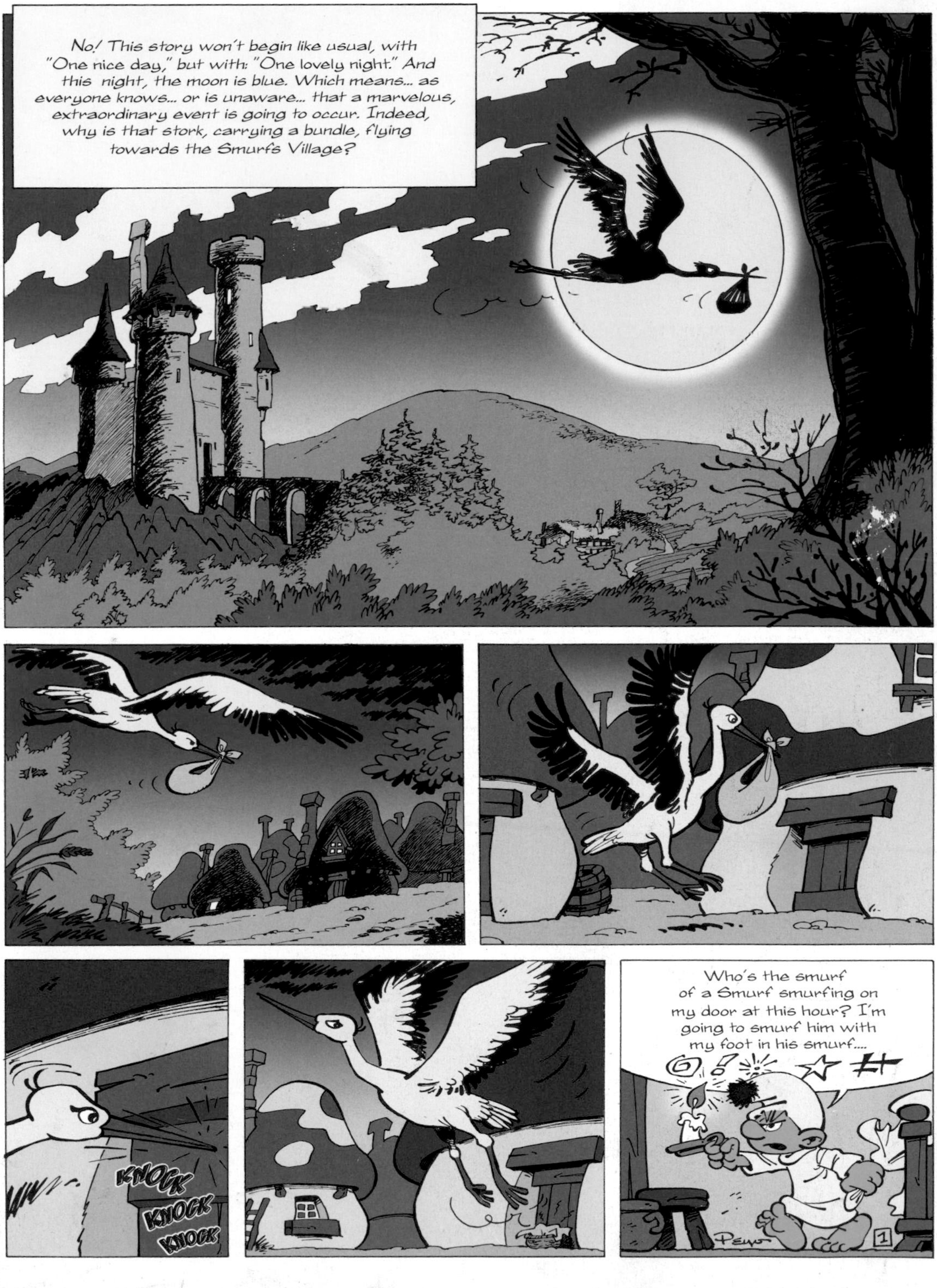

Peyo
No! This story won't begin like usual, with "One nice day," but with: "One lovely night." And this night, the moon is blue. Which means... as everyone knows... or is unaware... that a marvelous, extraordinary event is going to occur. Indeed, why is that stork, carrying a bundle, flying towards the Smurfs Village?
KNOCK
KNOCK
KNOCK
Who's the smurf of a Smurf smurfing on my door at this hour? I'm going to smurf him with my foot in his smurf....
Peyo
1

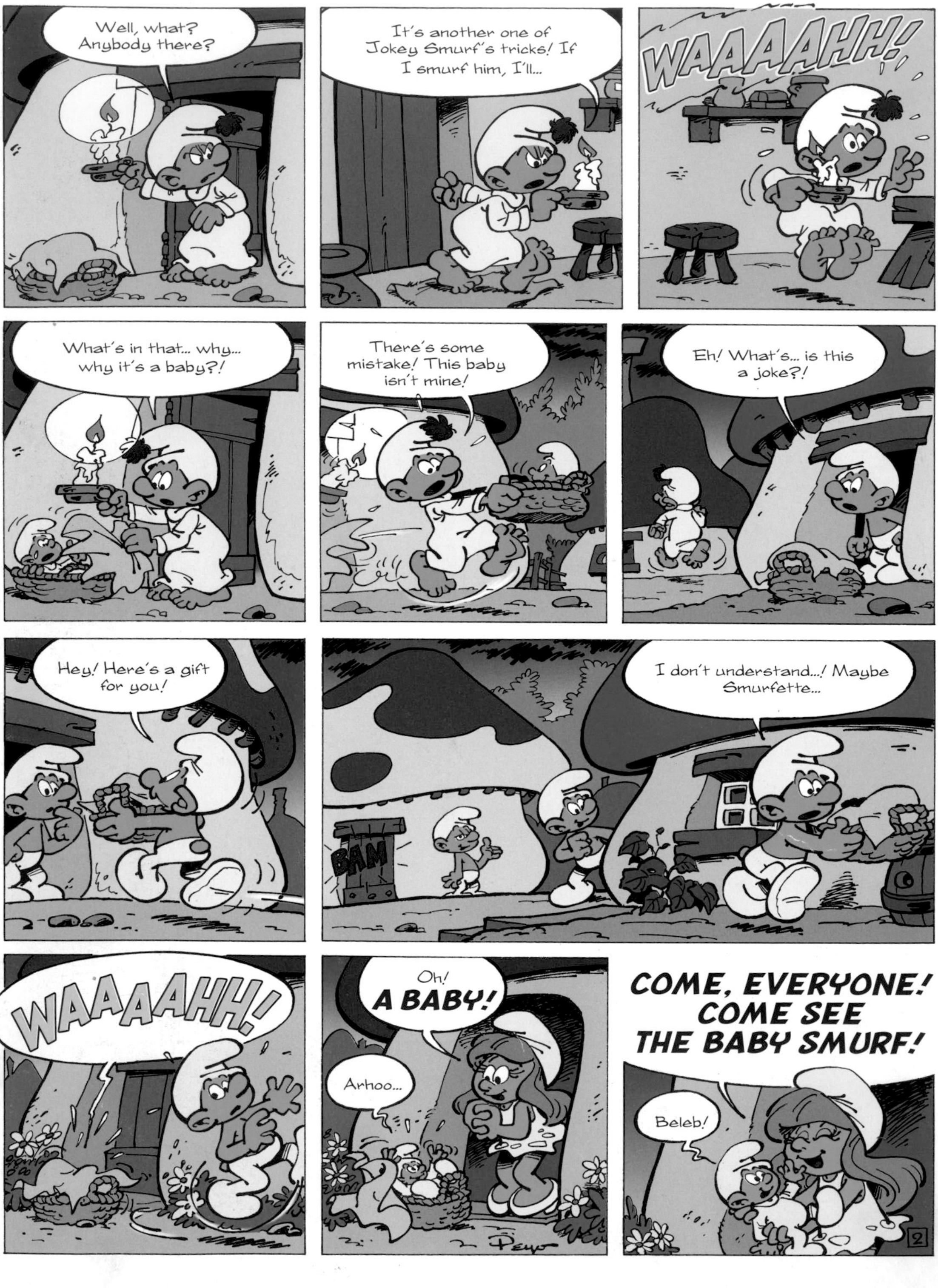
Well, what? Anybody there?
It's another one of Jokey Smurf's tricks! If I smurf him, I'll...
WAAAAAHH!
What's in that... why... why it's a baby?!
There's some mistake! This baby isn't mine!
Eh! What's... is this a joke?!
Hey! Here's a gift for you!
BAM
I don't understand...! Maybe Smurfette...
WAAAAAHH!
Oh!
A BABY!
Arhoo...
COME, EVERYONE! COME SEE THE BABY SMURF!
Beleb!
2

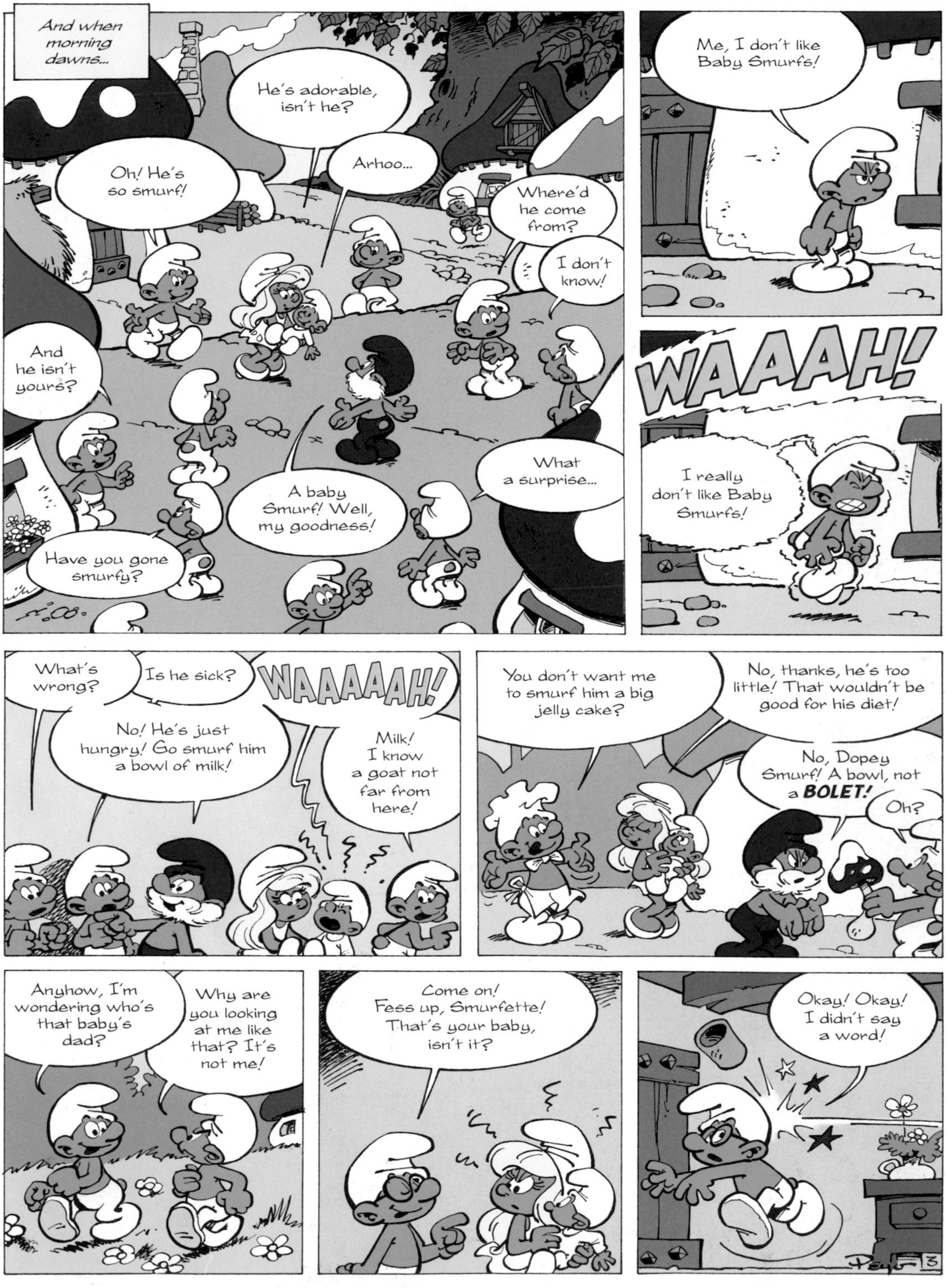
And when morning dawns...
He's adorable, isn't he?
Oh! He's so smurf!
Arhoo...
Where'd he come from?
I don't know!
And he isn't yours?
What a surprise...
A baby Smurf! Well, my goodness!
Have you gone smurfy?
Me, I don't like Baby Smurfs!
WAAAH!
I really don't like Baby Smurfs!
What's wrong?
Is he sick?
WAAAAAH!
No! He's just hungry! Go smurf him a bowl of milk!
Milk! I know a goat not far from here!
You don't want me to smurf him a big jelly cake?
No, thanks, he's too little! That wouldn't be good for his diet!
No, Dopey Smurf! A bowl, not a **BOLET!**
Oh?
Anyhow, I'm wondering who's that baby's dad?
Why are you looking at me like that? It's not me!
Come on! Fess up, Smurfette! That's your baby, isn't it?
Okay! Okay! I didn't say a word!

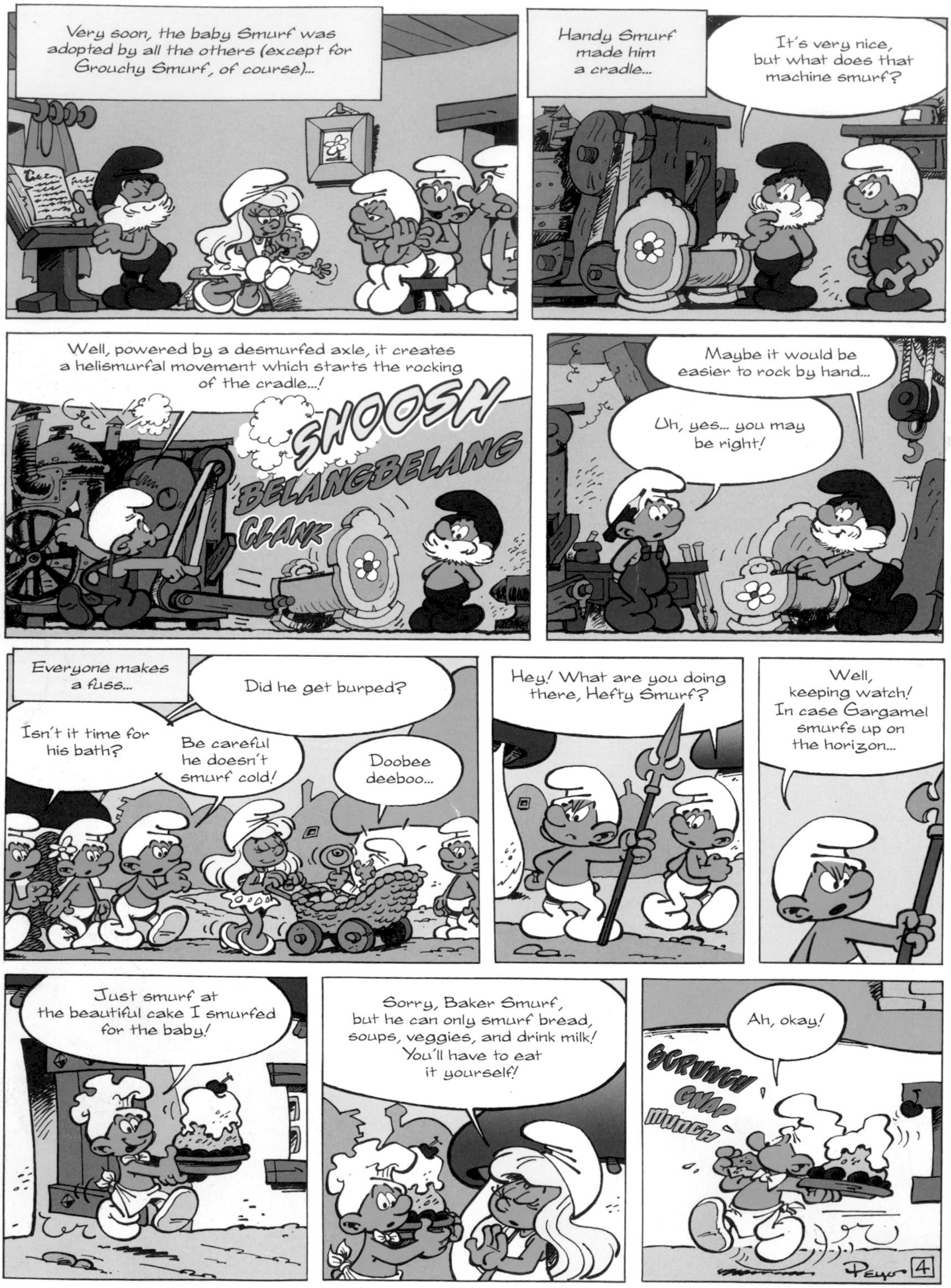
Very soon, the baby Smurf was adopted by all the others (except for Grouchy Smurf, of course)...
Handy Smurf made him a cradle...
It's very nice, but what does that machine smurf?
Well, powered by a desmurfed axle, it creates a helismurfal movement which starts the rocking of the cradle...!
SHOOSH
BELANGBELANG
CLANK
Maybe it would be easier to rock by hand...
Uh, yes... you may be right!
Everyone makes a fuss...
Did he get burped?
Isn't it time for his bath?
Be careful he doesn't smurf cold!
Doobee deeboo...
Hey! What are you doing there, Hefty Smurf?
Well, keeping watch! In case Gargamel smurfs up on the horizon...
Just smurf at the beautiful cake I smurfed for the baby!
Sorry, Baker Smurf, but he can only smurf bread, soups, veggies, and drink milk! You'll have to eat it yourself!
Ah, okay!
SCRUNCH
GNAP
MUNCH
Peyo
4

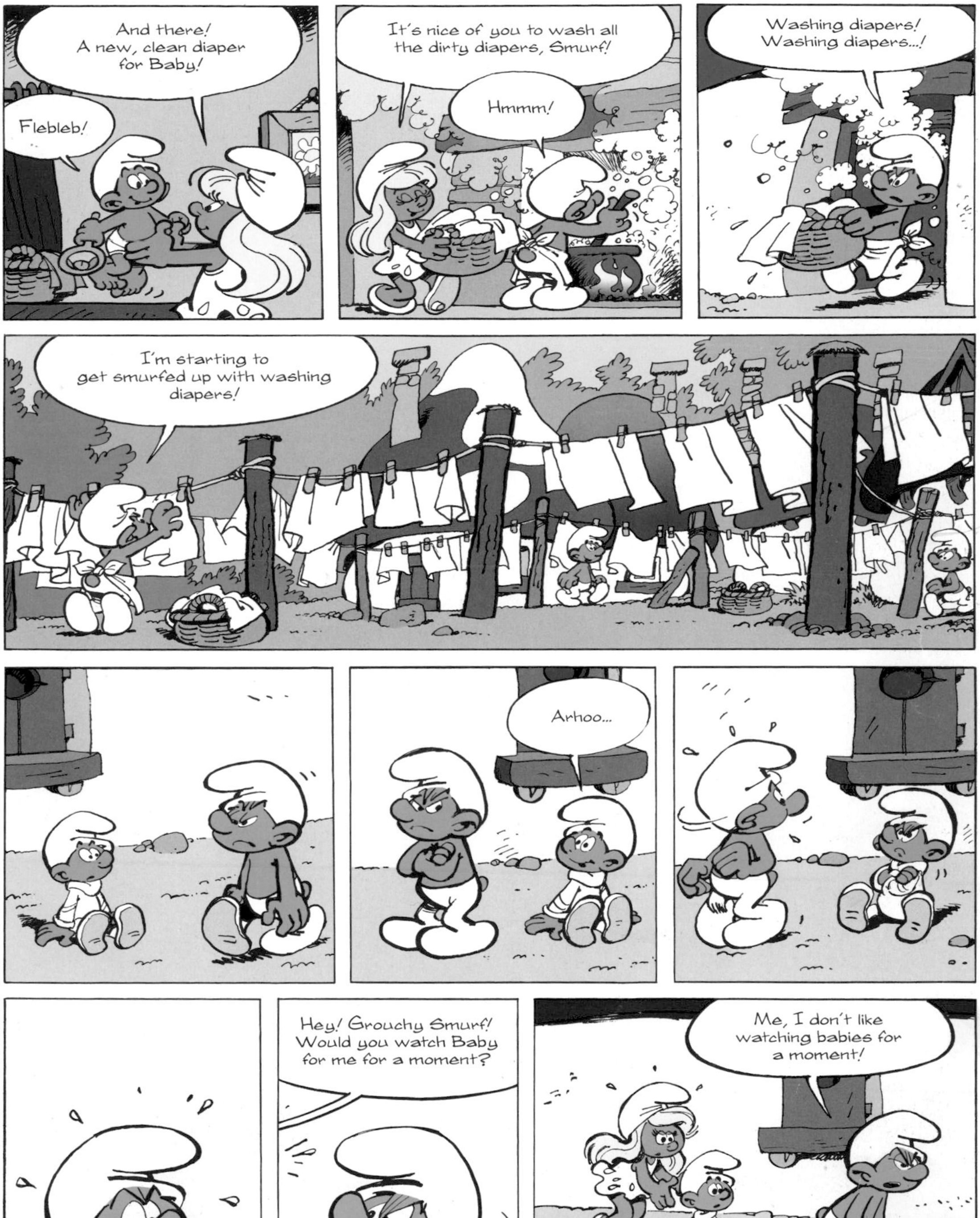
And there! A new, clean diaper for Baby!
Flebleb!
It's nice of you to wash all the dirty diapers, Smurf!
Hmmm!
Washing diapers! Washing diapers...!
I'm starting to get smurfed up with washing diapers!
Arhoo...
Hey! Grouchy Smurf! Would you watch Baby for me for a moment?
Me, I don't like watching babies for a moment!
Peyo
5

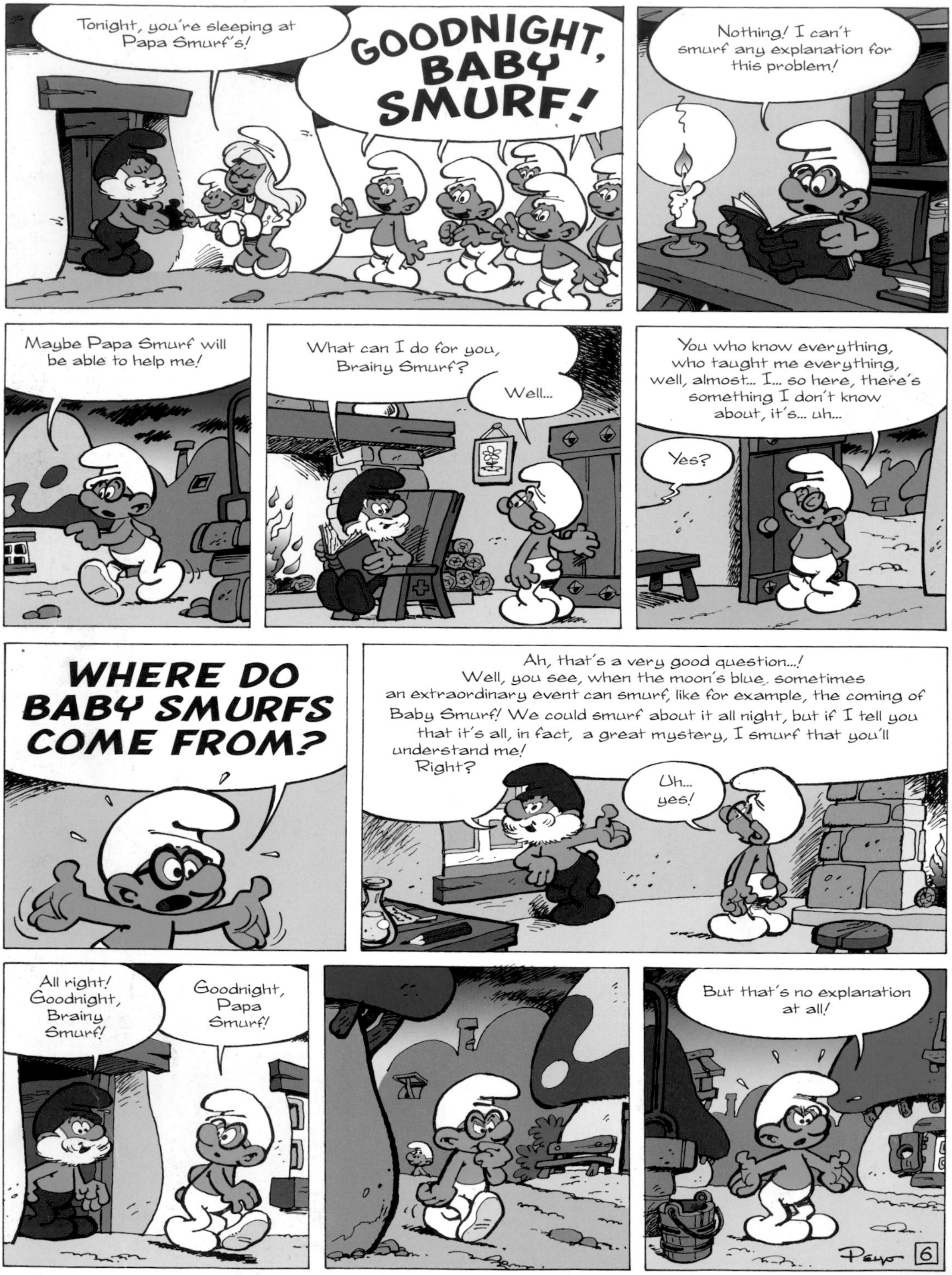

Tonight, you're sleeping at Papa Smurf's!
GOODNIGHT, BABY SMURF!
Nothing! I can't smurf any explanation for this problem!
Maybe Papa Smurf will be able to help me!
What can I do for you, Brainy Smurf?
Well...
You who know everything, who taught me everything, well, almost... I... so here, there's something I don't know about, it's... uh...
Yes?
WHERE DO BABY SMURFS COME FROM?
Ah, that's a very good question...! Well, you see, when the moon's blue, sometimes an extraordinary event can smurf, like for example, the coming of Baby Smurf! We could smurf about it all night, but if I tell you that it's all, in fact, a great mystery, I smurf that you'll understand me! Right?
Uh... yes!
All right! Goodnight, Brainy Smurf!
Goodnight, Papa Smurf!
But that's no explanation at all!
Peyo
6

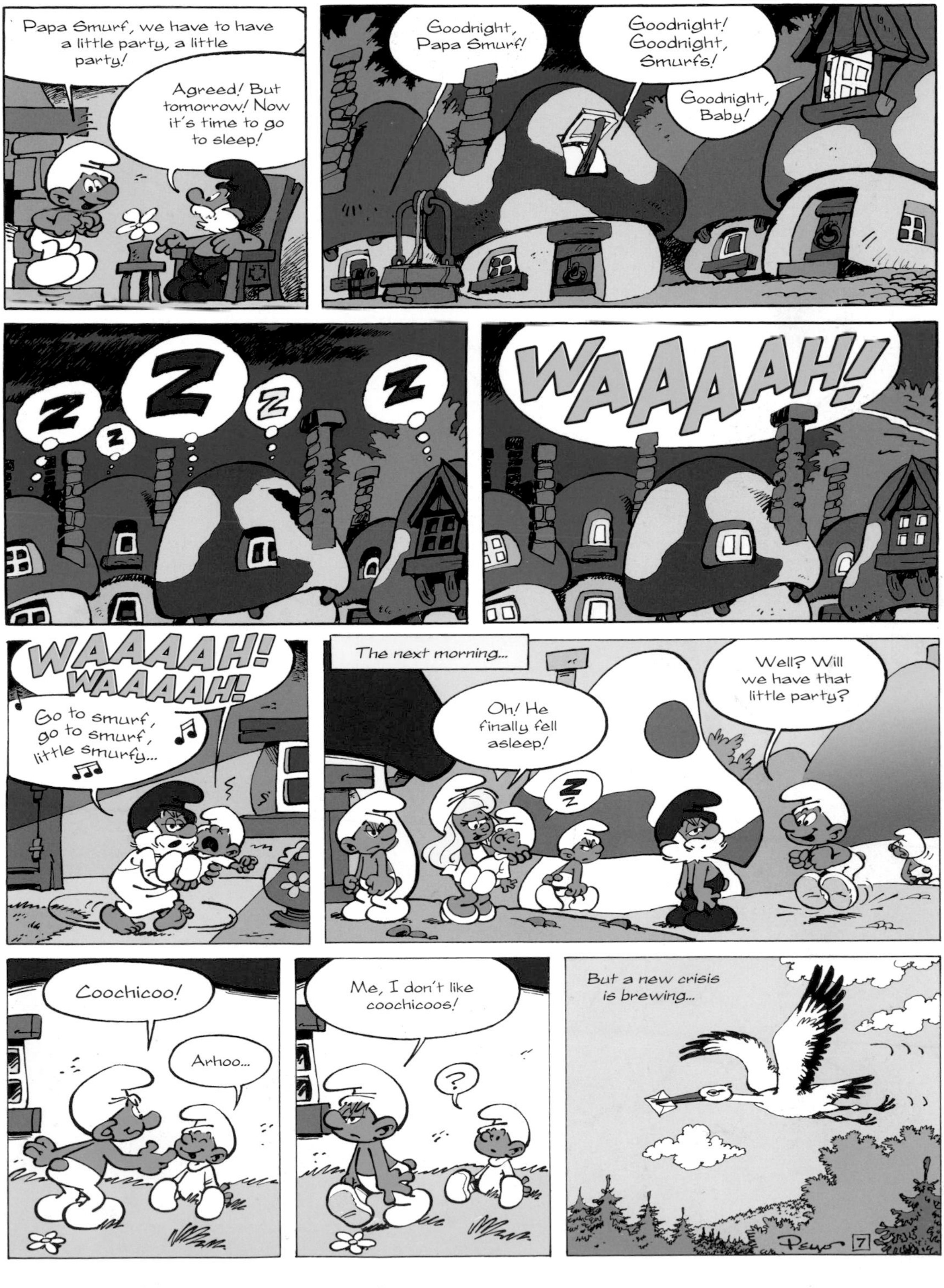
Papa Smurf, we have to have a little party, a little party!
Agreed! But tomorrow! Now it's time to go to sleep!
Goodnight, Papa Smurf!
Goodnight! Goodnight, Smurfs!
Goodnight, Baby!
Z
Z
Z
Z
Z
WAAAAH!
WAAAAH! WAAAAH!
Go to smurf, go to smurf, little smurfy...
The next morning...
Oh! He finally fell asleep!
Z
Well? Will we have that little party?
Coochicoo!
Arhoo...
Me, I don't like coochicoos!
?
But a new crisis is brewing...
Peyo
7

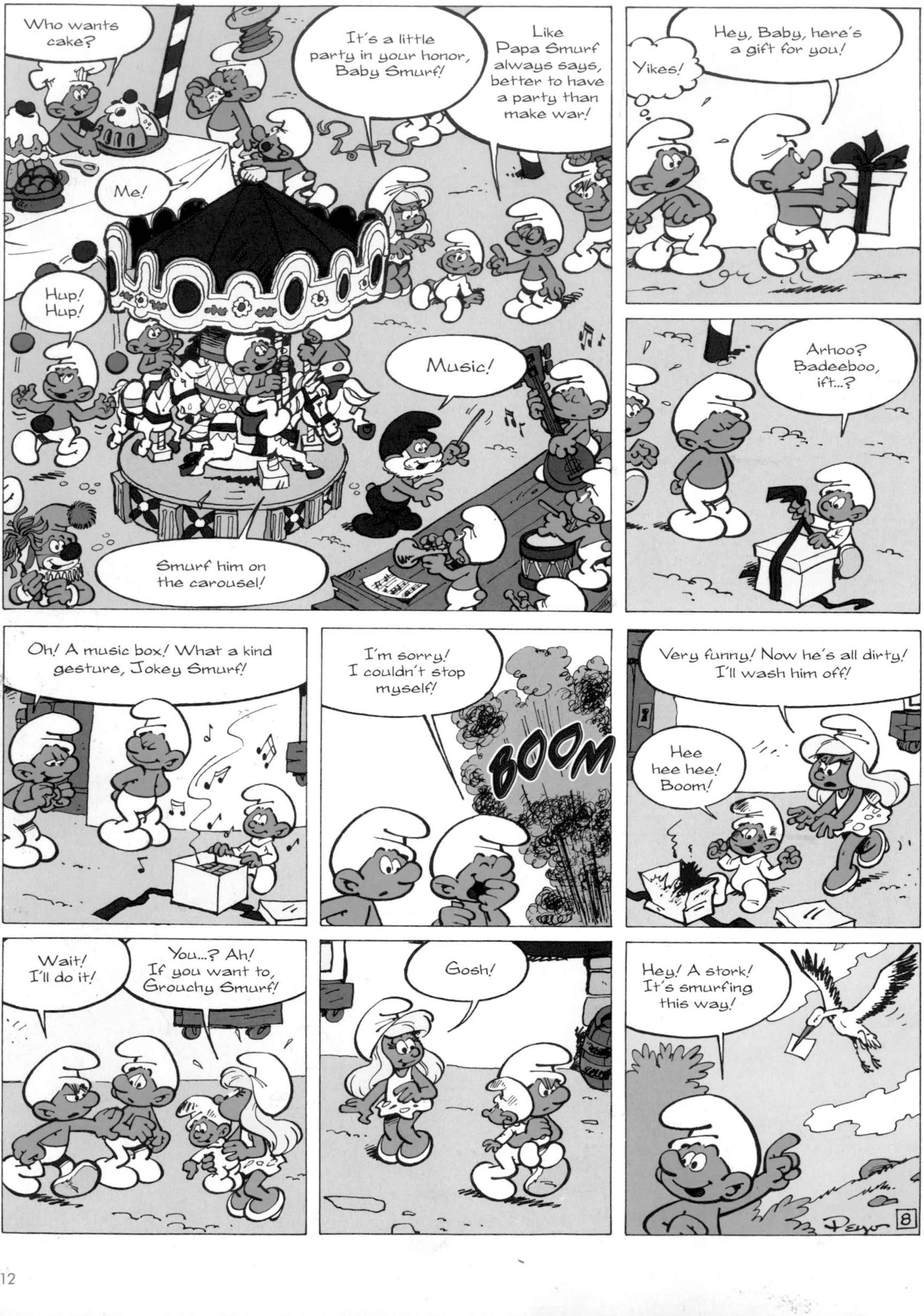

Who wants cake?
It's a little party in your honor, Baby Smurf!
Like Papa Smurf always says, better to have a party than make war!
Me!
Hup! Hup!
Music!
Smurf him on the carousel!
Yikes!
Hey, Baby, here's a gift for you!
Arhoo? Badeeboo, ift...?
Oh! A music box! What a kind gesture, Jokey Smurf!
I'm sorry! I couldn't stop myself!
BOOM
Very funny! Now he's all dirty! I'll wash him off!
Hee hee hee! Boom!
Wait! I'll do it!
You...? Ah! If you want to, Grouchy Smurf!
Gosh!
Hey! A stork! It's smurfing this way!
8

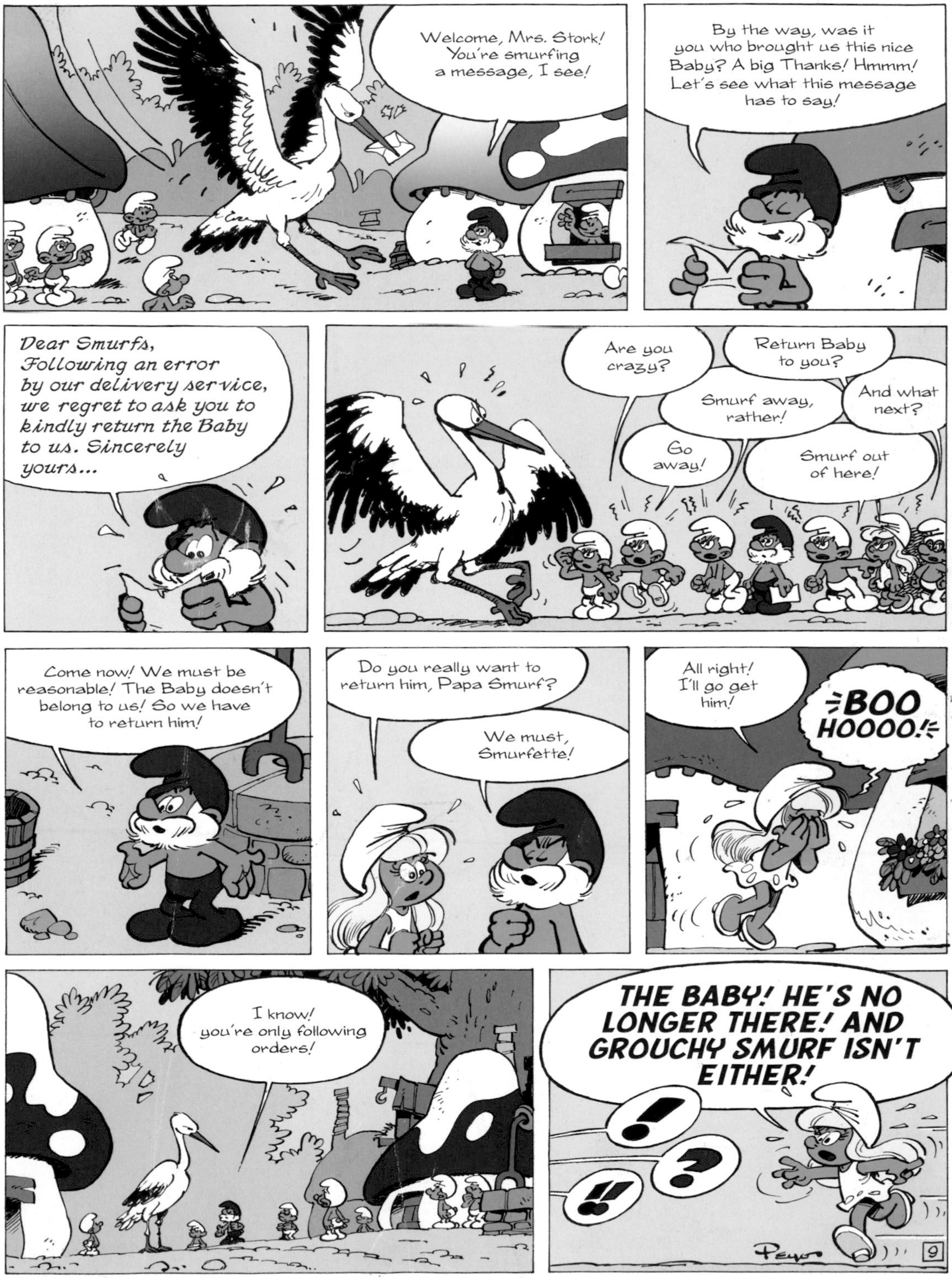

Welcome, Mrs. Stork! You're smurfing a message, I see!
By the way, was it you who brought us this nice Baby? A big Thanks! Hmmm! Let's see what this message has to say!
Dear Smurfs, Following an error by our delivery service, we regret to ask you to kindly return the Baby to us. Sincerely yours...
Are you crazy?
Return Baby to you?
Smurf away, rather!
And what next?
Go away!
Smurf out of here!
Come now! We must be reasonable! The Baby doesn't belong to us! So we have to return him!
Do you really want to return him, Papa Smurf?
We must, Smurfette!
All right! I'll go get him!
BOO HOOOO!
I know! you're only following orders!
THE BABY! HE'S NO LONGER THERE! AND GROUCHY SMURF ISN'T EITHER!
!
?
!!
Peyo
9

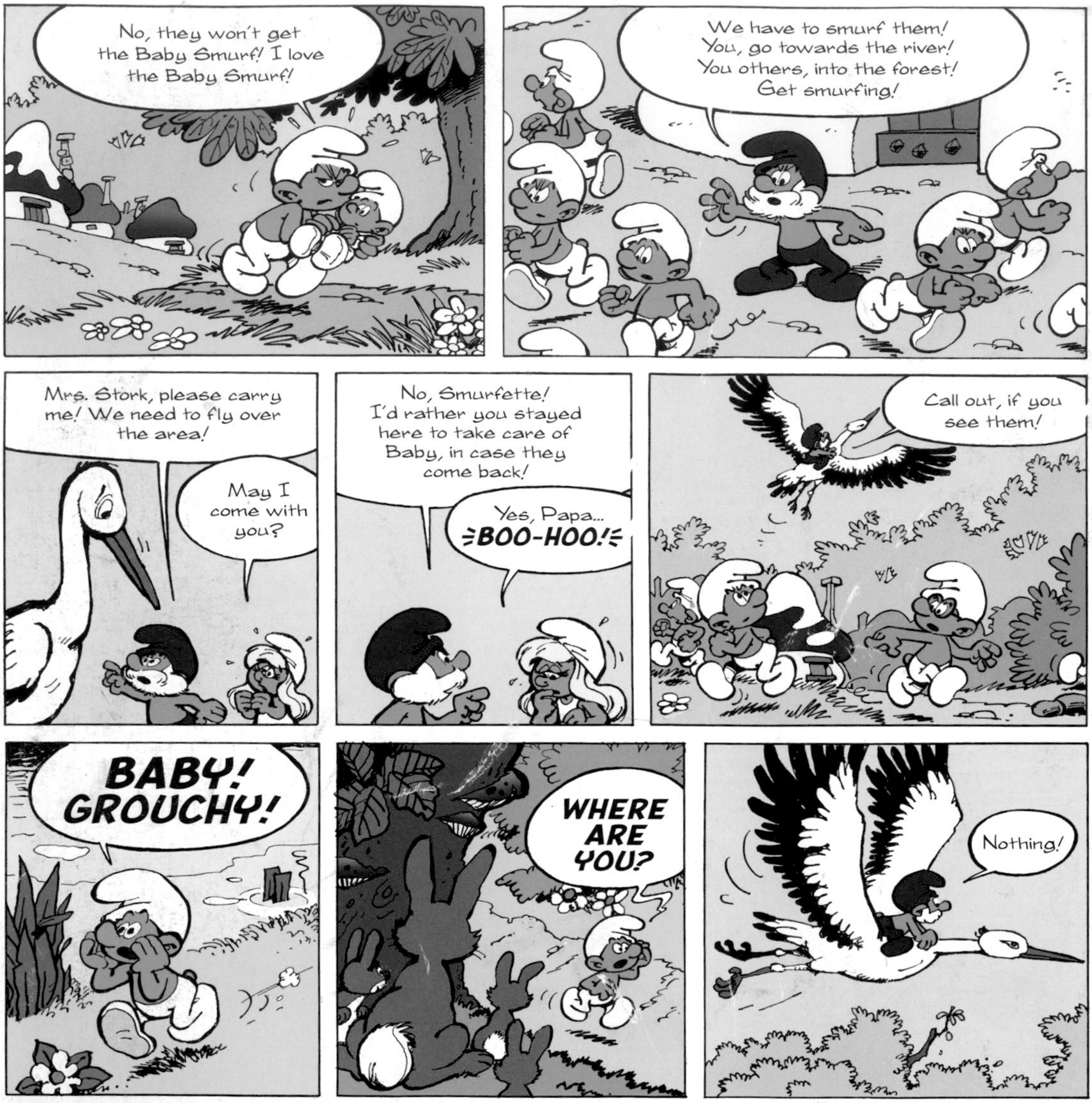
No, they won't get the Baby Smurf! I love the Baby Smurf!
We have to smurf them! You, go towards the river! You others, into the forest! Get smurfing!
Mrs. Stork, please carry me! We need to fly over the area!
May I come with you?
No, Smurfette! I'd rather you stayed here to take care of Baby, in case they come back!
Yes, Papa... BOO-HOO!
Call out, if you see them!
BABY! GROUCHY!
WHERE ARE YOU?
Nothing!
YOOHOO!
Arflebleb...
Shh!
YOOHOO!
Yoohoo!

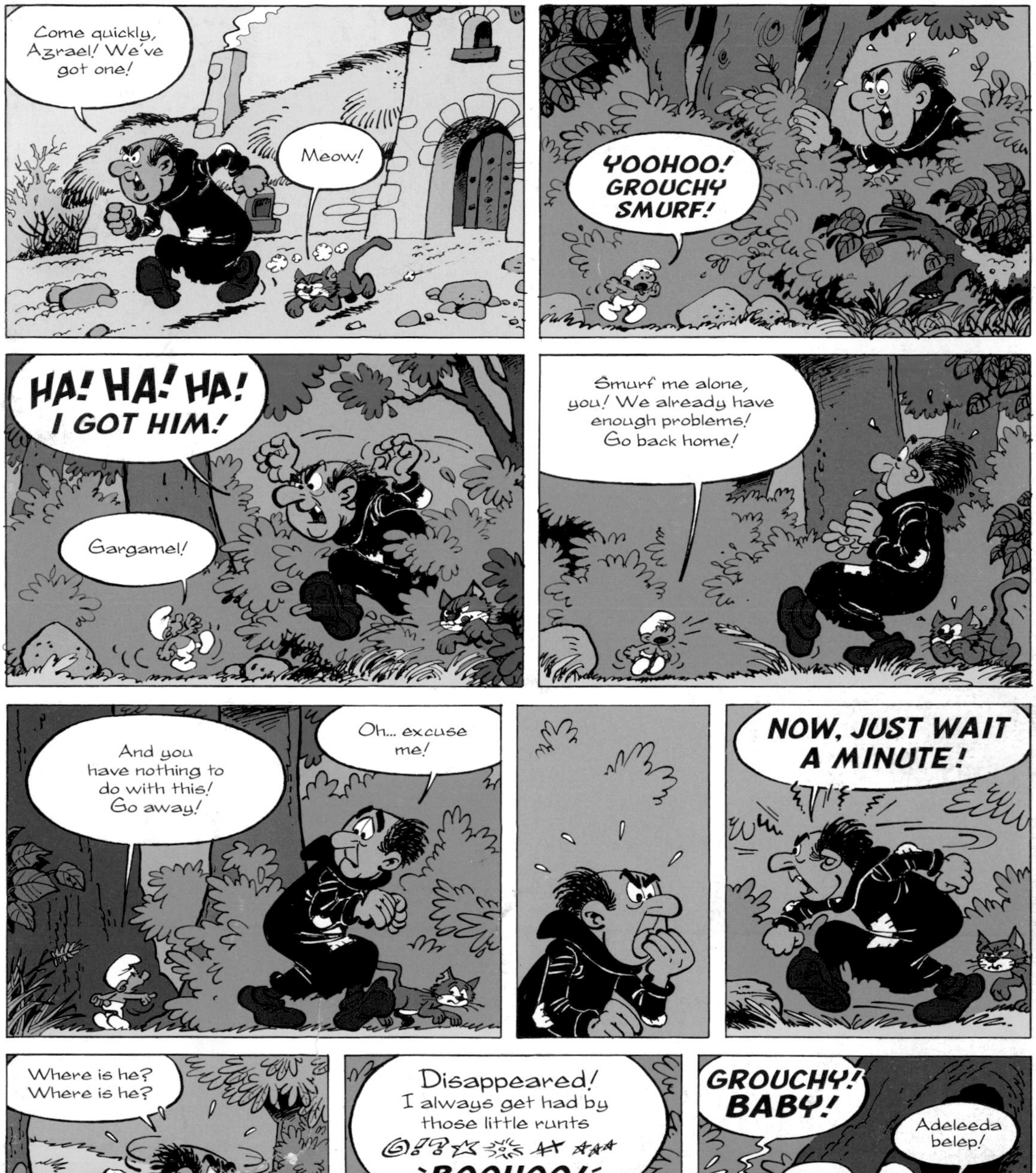

Come quickly, Azrael! We've got one!
Meow!
YOOHOO! GROUCHY SMURF!
HA! HA! HA! I GOT HIM!
Gargamel!
Smurf me alone, you! We already have enough problems! Go back home!
And you have nothing to do with this! Go away!
Oh... excuse me!
NOW, JUST WAIT A MINUTE!
Where is he? Where is he?
Disappeared! I always get had by those little runts
BOOHOO!
GROUCHY! BABY!
Adeleeda belep!
Hush!

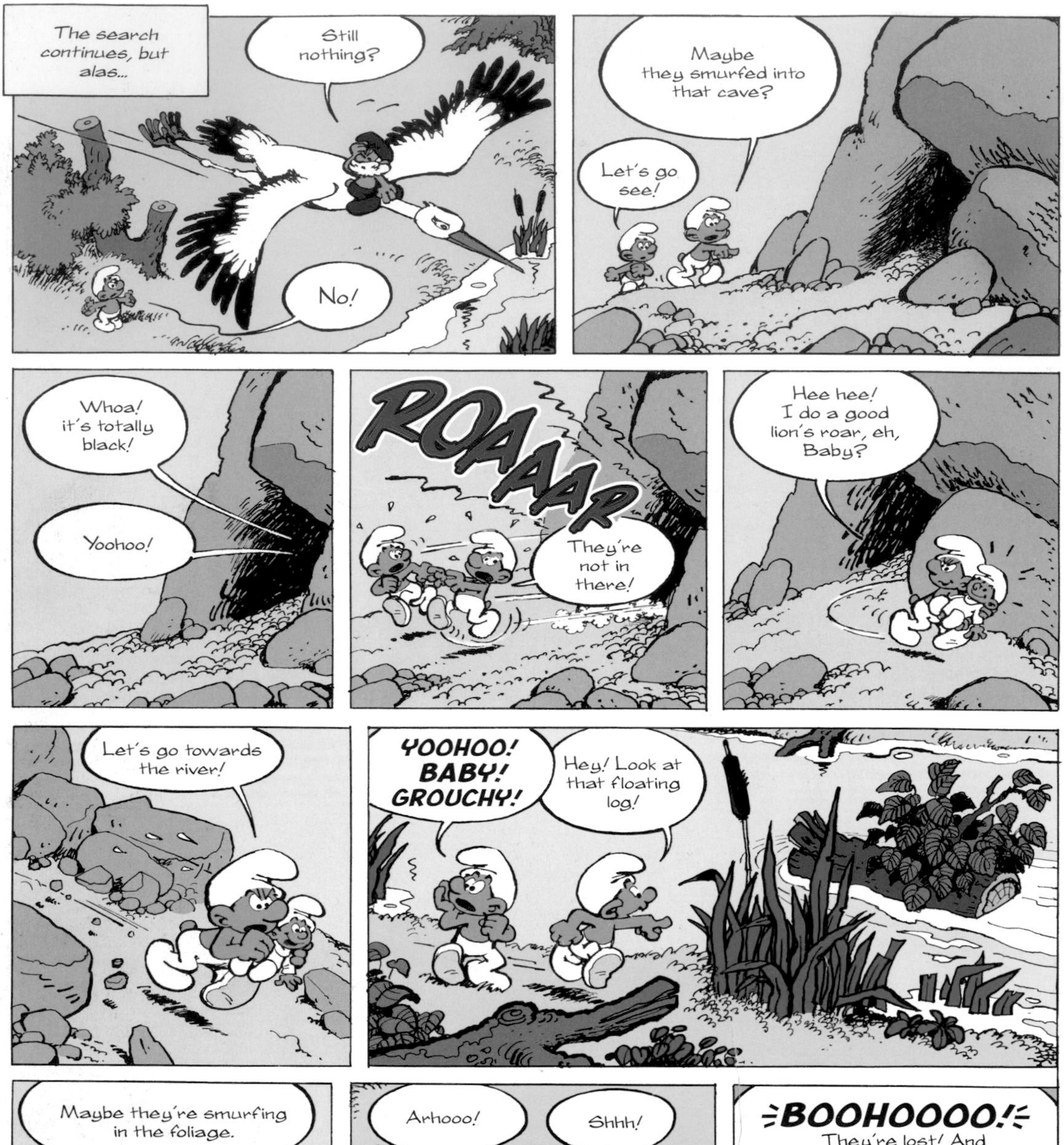

The search continues, but alas...
Still nothing?
No!
Maybe they smurfed into that cave?
Let's go see!
Whoa! it's totally black!
Yoohoo!
ROAAAAR
They're not in there!
Hee hee! I do a good lion's roar, eh, Baby?
Let's go towards the river!
YOOHOO! BABY! GROUCHY!
Hey! Look at that floating log!
Maybe they're smurfing in the foliage.
No way...! Come on! Let's keep looking!
Arhooo!
Shhh!
BOOHOOOO! They're lost! And the Baby's going to die! SOB!
Peyo
12

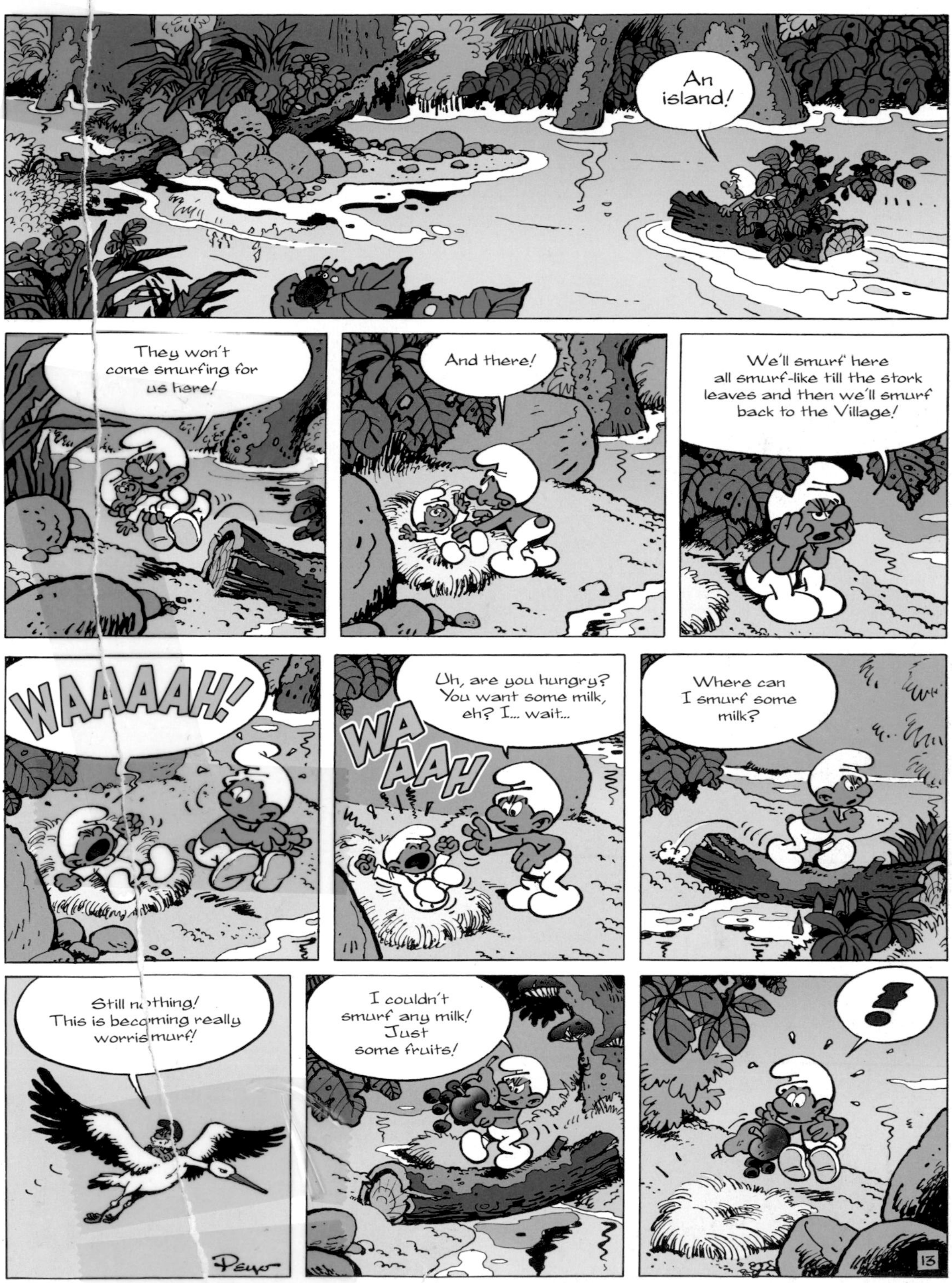

An island!
They won't come smurfing for us here!
And there!
We'll smurf here all smurf-like till the stork leaves and then we'll smurf back to the Village!
WAAAAAH!
WA AAH
Uh, are you hungry? You want some milk, eh? I... wait...
Where can I smurf some milk?
Still nothing! This is becoming really worrismurf!
I couldn't smurf any milk! Just some fruits!
!
Peyo
13

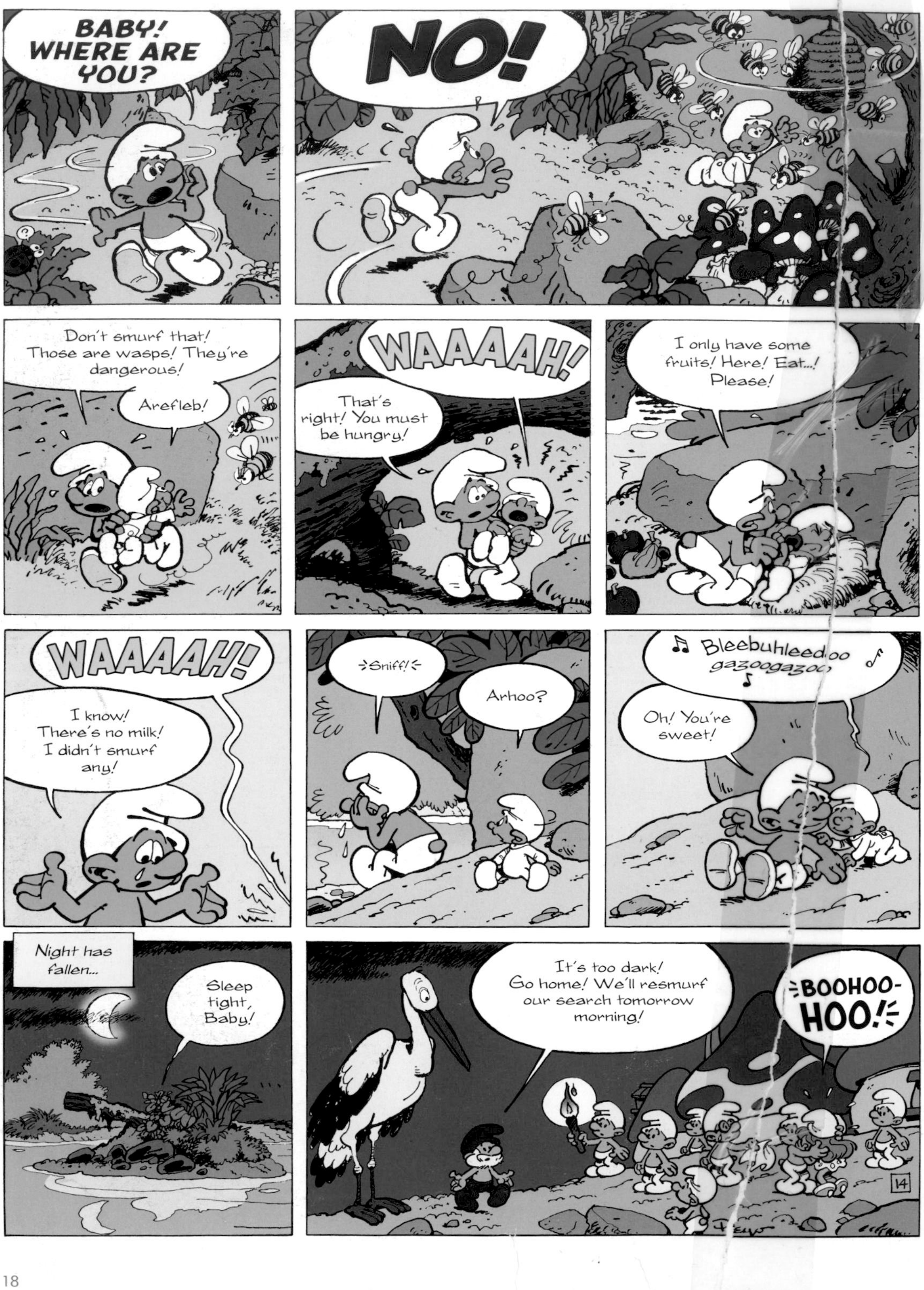

BABY! WHERE ARE YOU?
NO!
Don't smurf that! Those are wasps! They're dangerous!
Arefleb!
WAAAAH!
That's right! You must be hungry!
I only have some fruits! Here! Eat...! Please!
WAAAAH!
I know! There's no milk! I didn't smurf any!
Sniff!
Arhoo?
Bleebuhleedoo gazoogazoo
Oh! You're sweet!
Night has fallen...
Sleep tight, Baby!
It's too dark! Go home! We'll resmurf our search tomorrow morning!
BOOHOO-HOO!
14

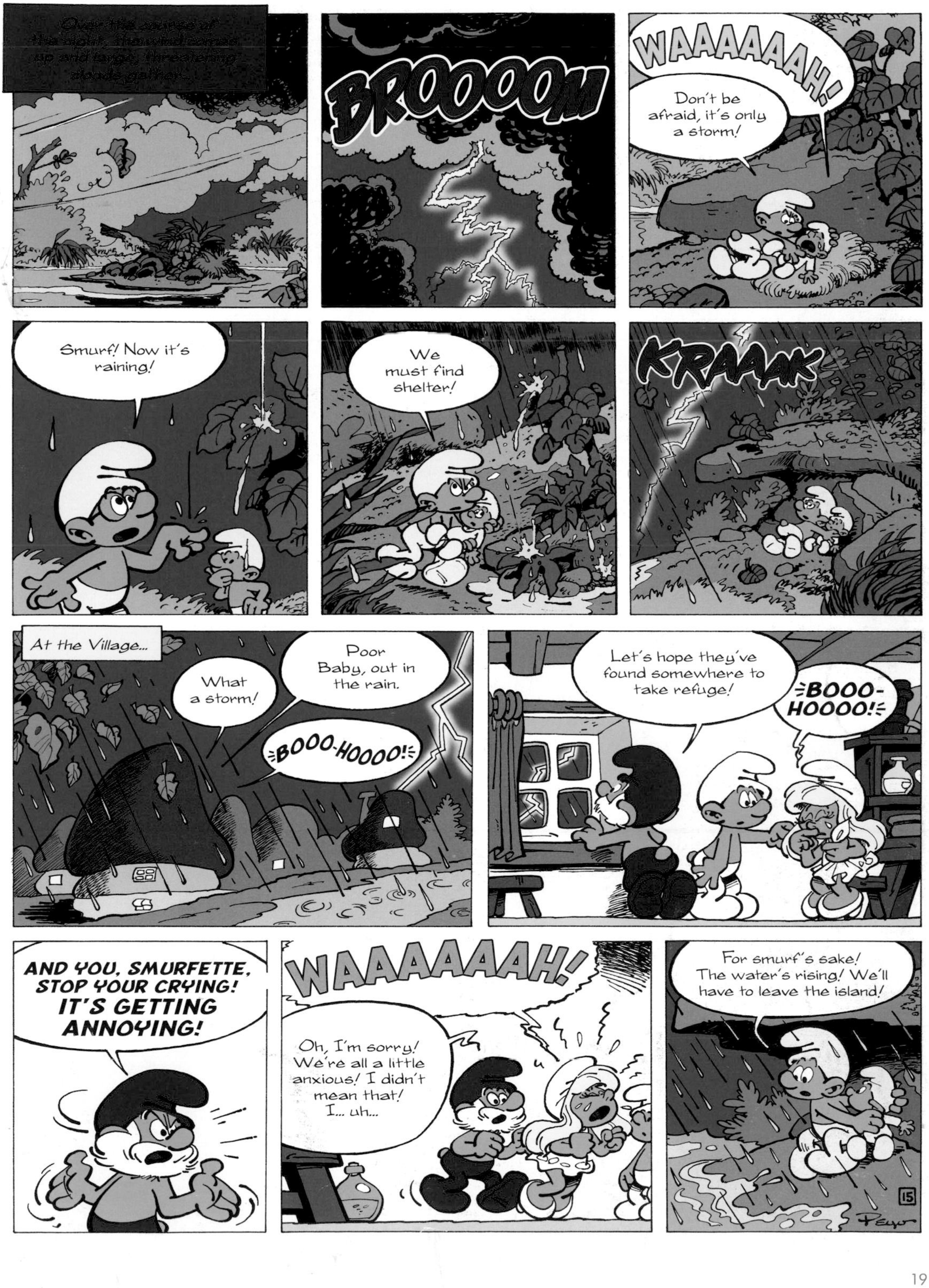

[redacted]
BROOOOM
WAAAAAAH!
Don't be afraid, it's only a storm!
Smurf! Now it's raining!
We must find shelter!
KRAAAK
At the Village...
What a storm!
Poor Baby, out in the rain.
BOOO-HOOOO!
Let's hope they've found somewhere to take refuge!
BOOO-HOOOO!
AND YOU, SMURFETTE, STOP YOUR CRYING! IT'S GETTING ANNOYING!
WAAAAAAAH!
Oh, I'm sorry! We're all a little anxious! I didn't mean that! I... uh...
For smurf's sake! The water's rising! We'll have to leave the island!
15

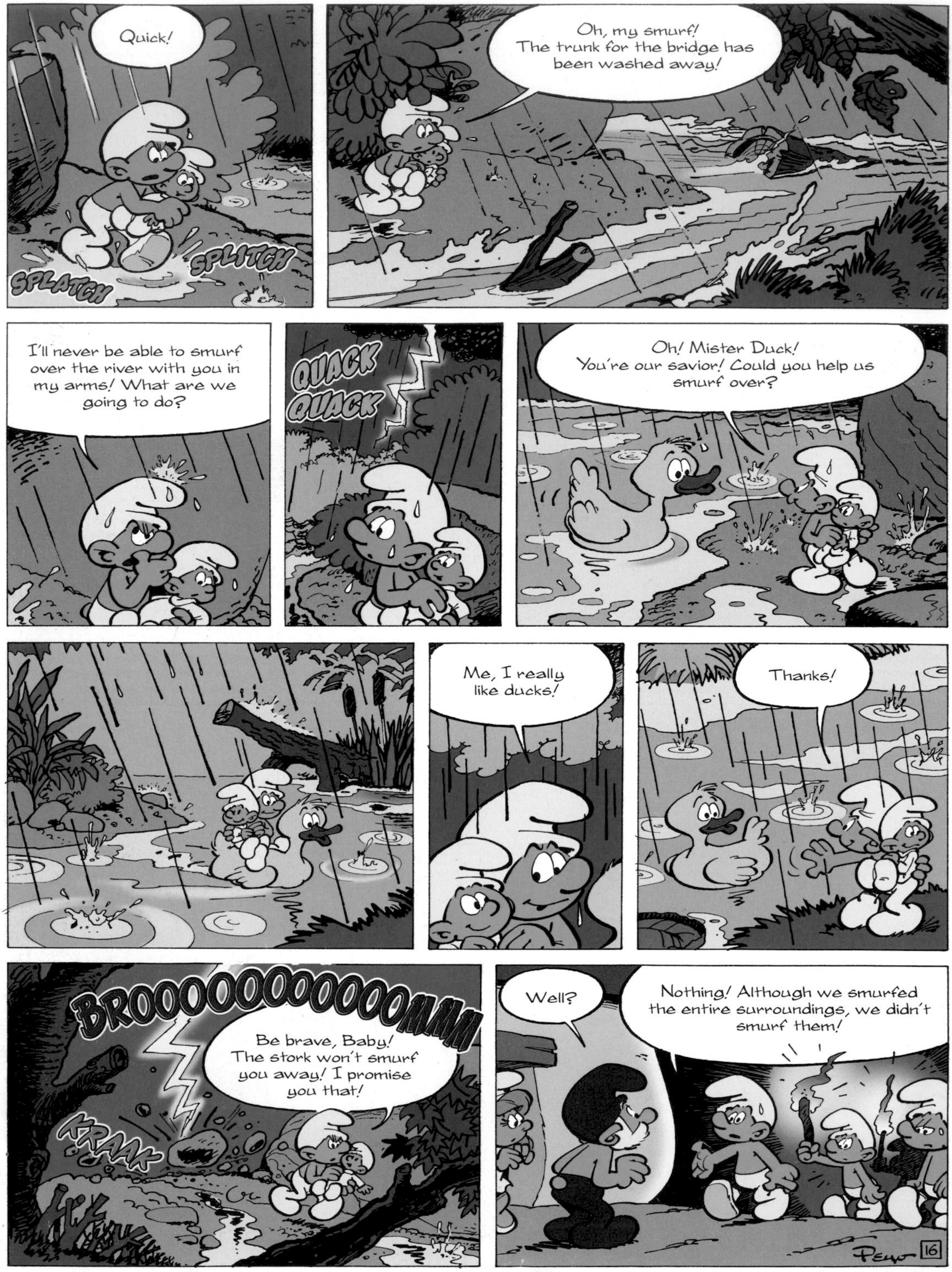
Quick!
SPLATCH
SPLITCH
Oh, my smurf! The trunk for the bridge has been washed away!
I'll never be able to smurf over the river with you in my arms! What are we going to do?
QUACK QUACK
Oh! Mister Duck! You're our savior! Could you help us smurf over?
Me, I really like ducks!
Thanks!
BROOOOOOOOOOOMMM
Be brave, Baby! The stork won't smurf you away! I promise you that!
KRAAK
Well?
Nothing! Although we smurfed the entire surroundings, we didn't smurf them!
Peyo
16

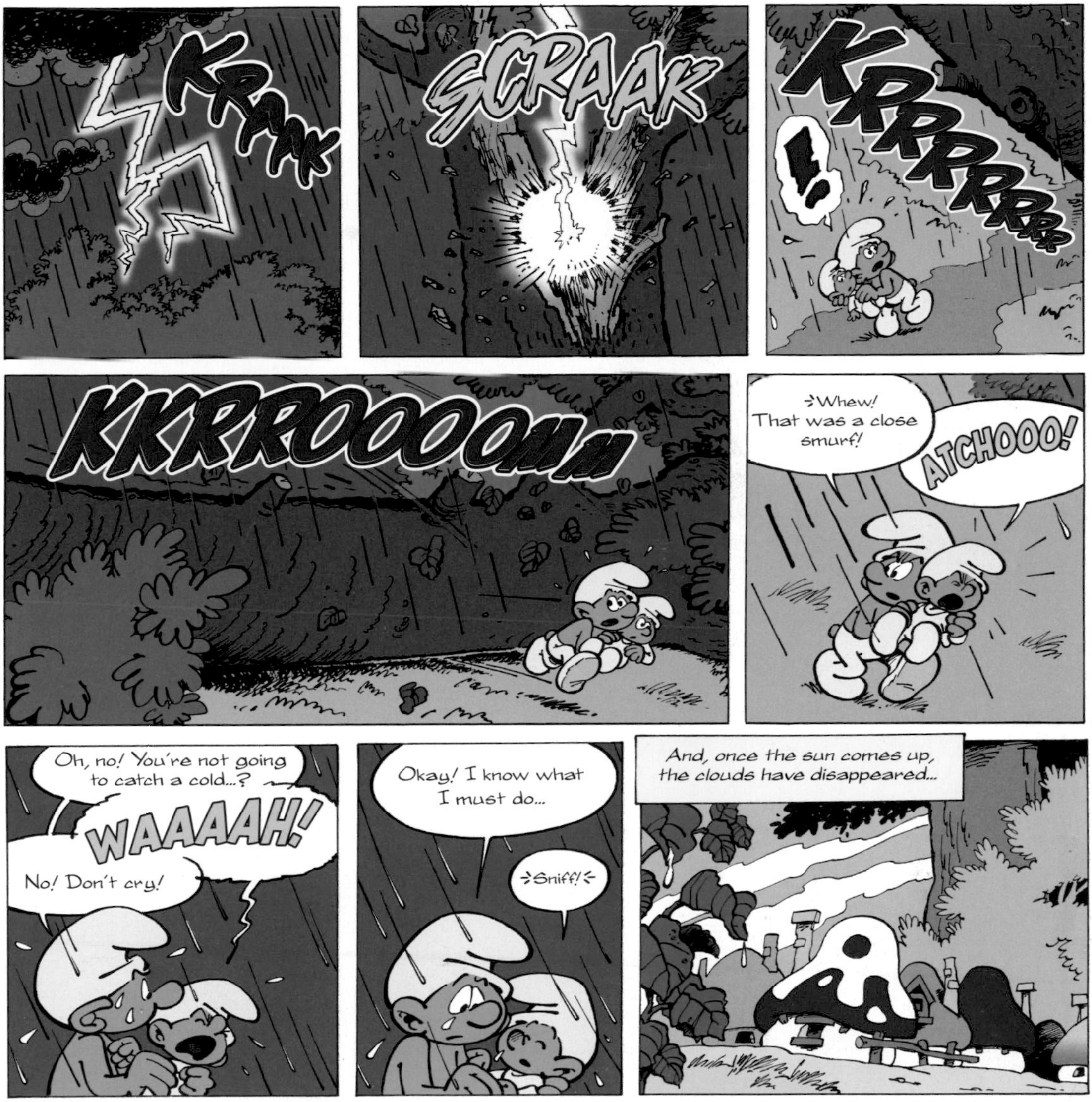
KRAAK
SCRAAK
KRRRRRRRR
!
KKRROOOOMM
Whew! That was a close smurf!
ATCHOOO!
Oh, no! You're not going to catch a cold...?
WAAAAH!
No! Don't cry!
Okay! I know what I must do...
Sniff!
And, once the sun comes up, the clouds have disappeared...
Still nothing! I fear the worst!
No, I won't cry. No, I won't cry.
AGOOGLE PEETEEPOOO ARHOO!
!?
17
Peyo

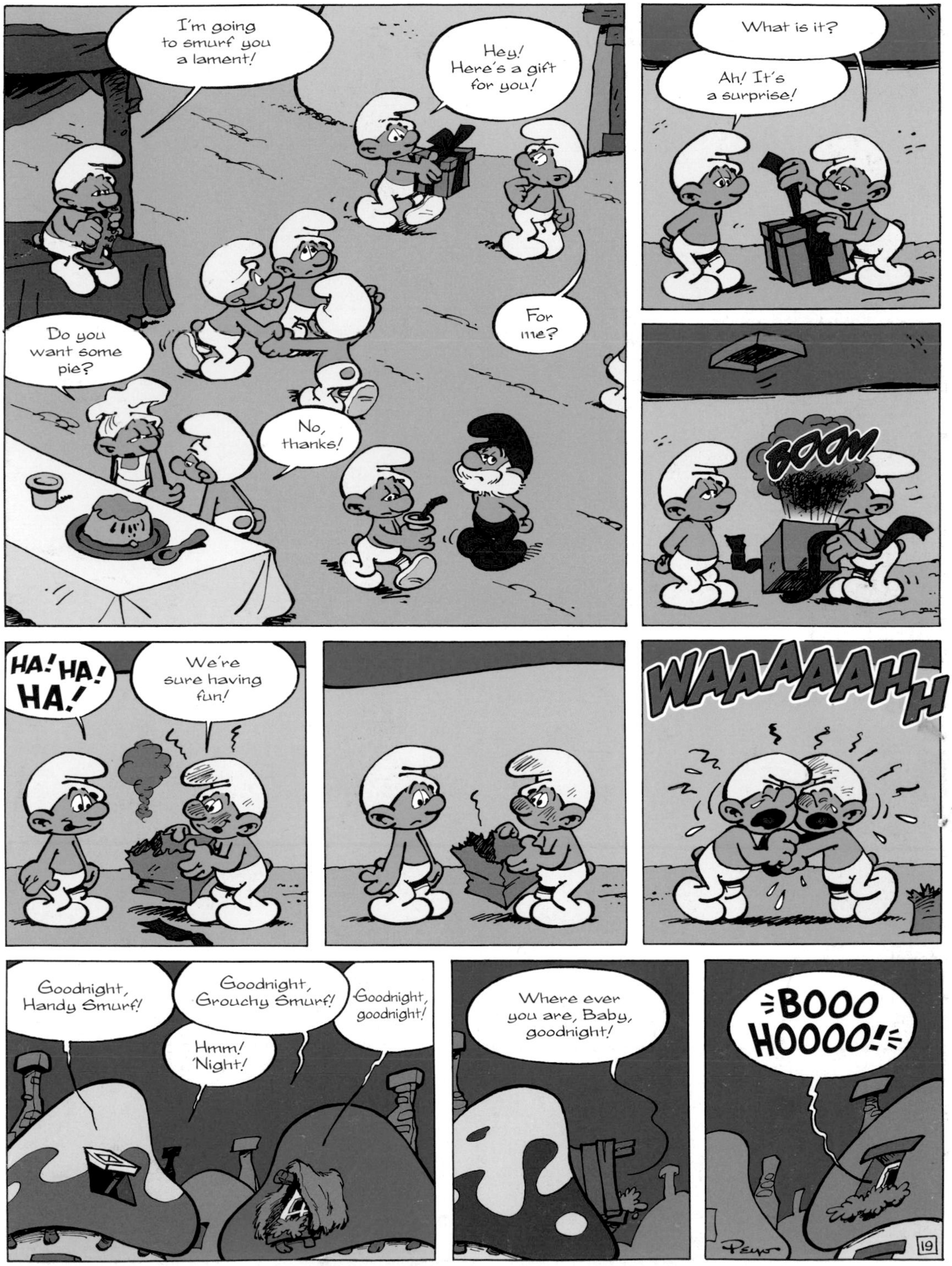

I'm going to smurf you a lament!
Hey! Here's a gift for you!
For me?
Do you want some pie?
No, thanks!
What is it?
Ah! It's a surprise!
BOOM
HA! HA! HA!
We're sure having fun!
WAAAAAHH
Goodnight, Handy Smurf!
Goodnight, Grouchy Smurf!
Hmm! 'Night!
Goodnight, goodnight!
Where ever you are, Baby, goodnight!
BOOO HOOOO!
Peyo
19

A SMURFING PARTY

28

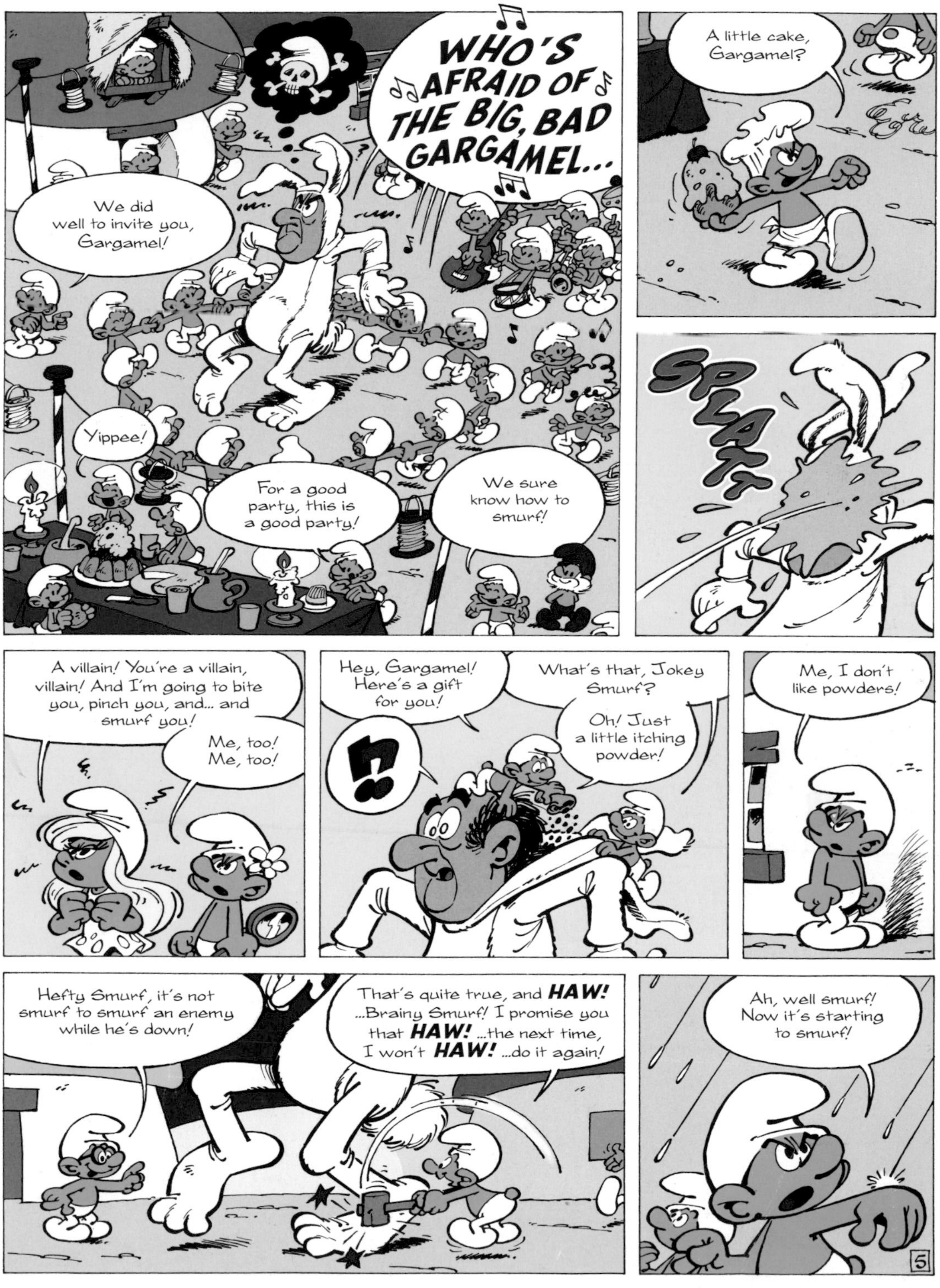
WHO'S AFRAID OF THE BIG, BAD GARGAMEL...
We did well to invite you, Gargamel!
Yippee!
For a good party, this is a good party!
We sure know how to smurf!
A little cake, Gargamel?
SPLATT
A villain! You're a villain, villain! And I'm going to bite you, pinch you, and... and smurf you!
Me, too! Me, too!
Hey, Gargamel! Here's a gift for you!
What's that, Jokey Smurf?
Oh! Just a little itching powder!
Me, I don't like powders!
Hefty Smurf, it's not smurf to smurf an enemy while he's down!
That's quite true, and HAW! ...Brainy Smurf! I promise you that HAW! ...the next time, I won't HAW! ...do it again!
Ah, well smurf! Now it's starting to smurf!
5

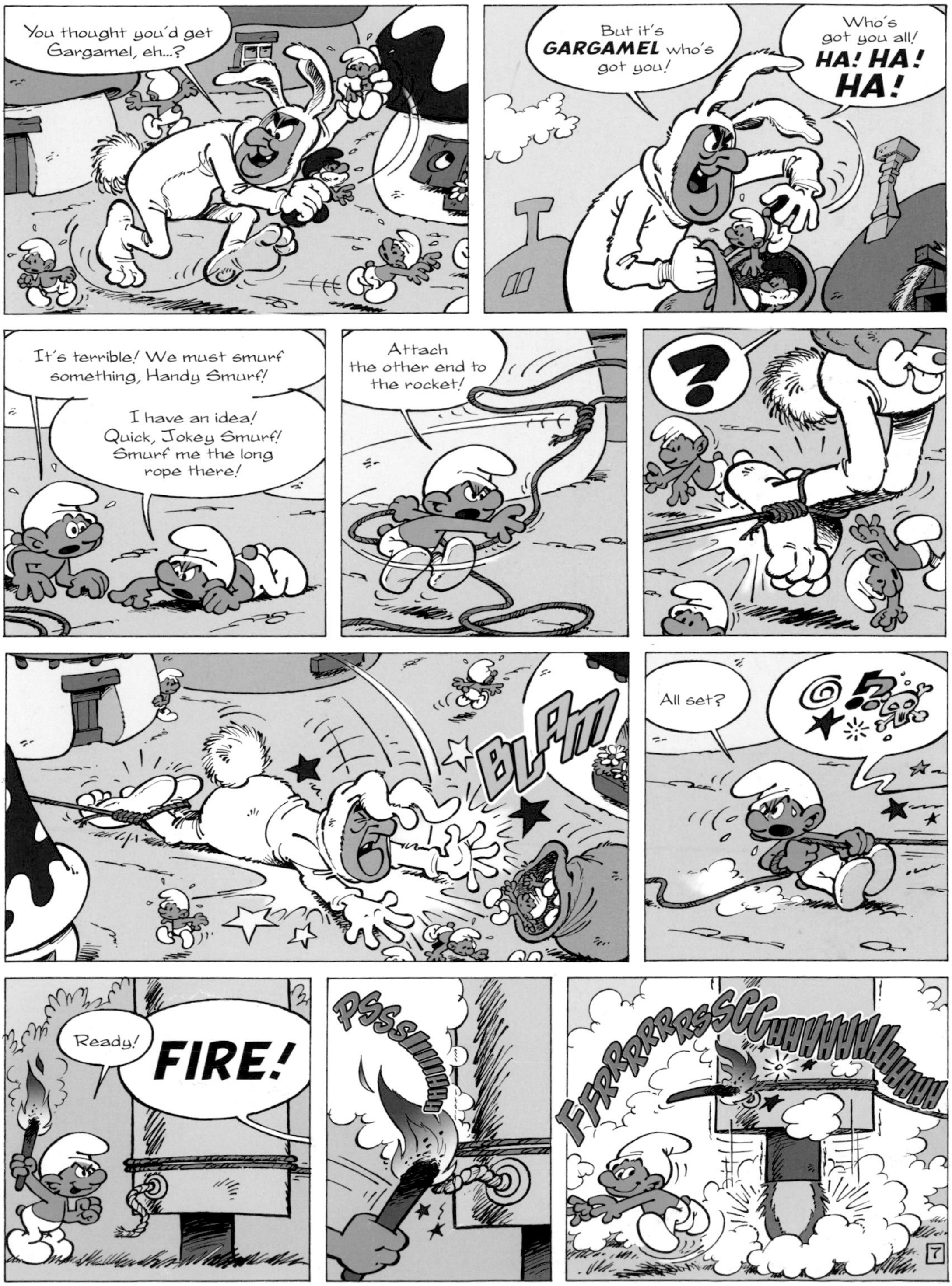
You thought you'd get Gargamel, eh...?
But it's GARGAMEL who's got you!
Who's got you all! HA! HA! HA!
It's terrible! We must smurf something, Handy Smurf!
I have an idea! Quick, Jokey Smurf! Smurf me the long rope there!
Attach the other end to the rocket!
?
BLAM
All set?
Ready!
FIRE!
PSSSHHHHHH
FFRRRRRRSSCCHHHHHHHHHHHHHH
7

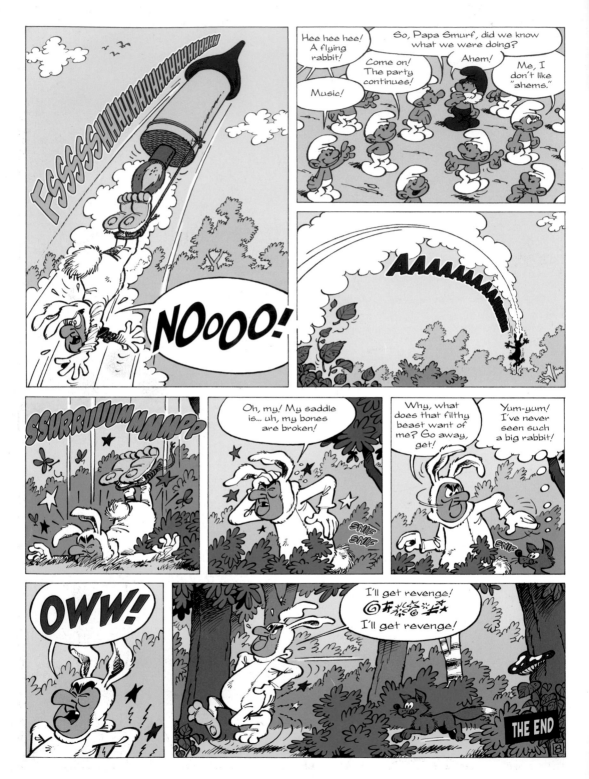

THE WEATHER-SMURFING MACHINE

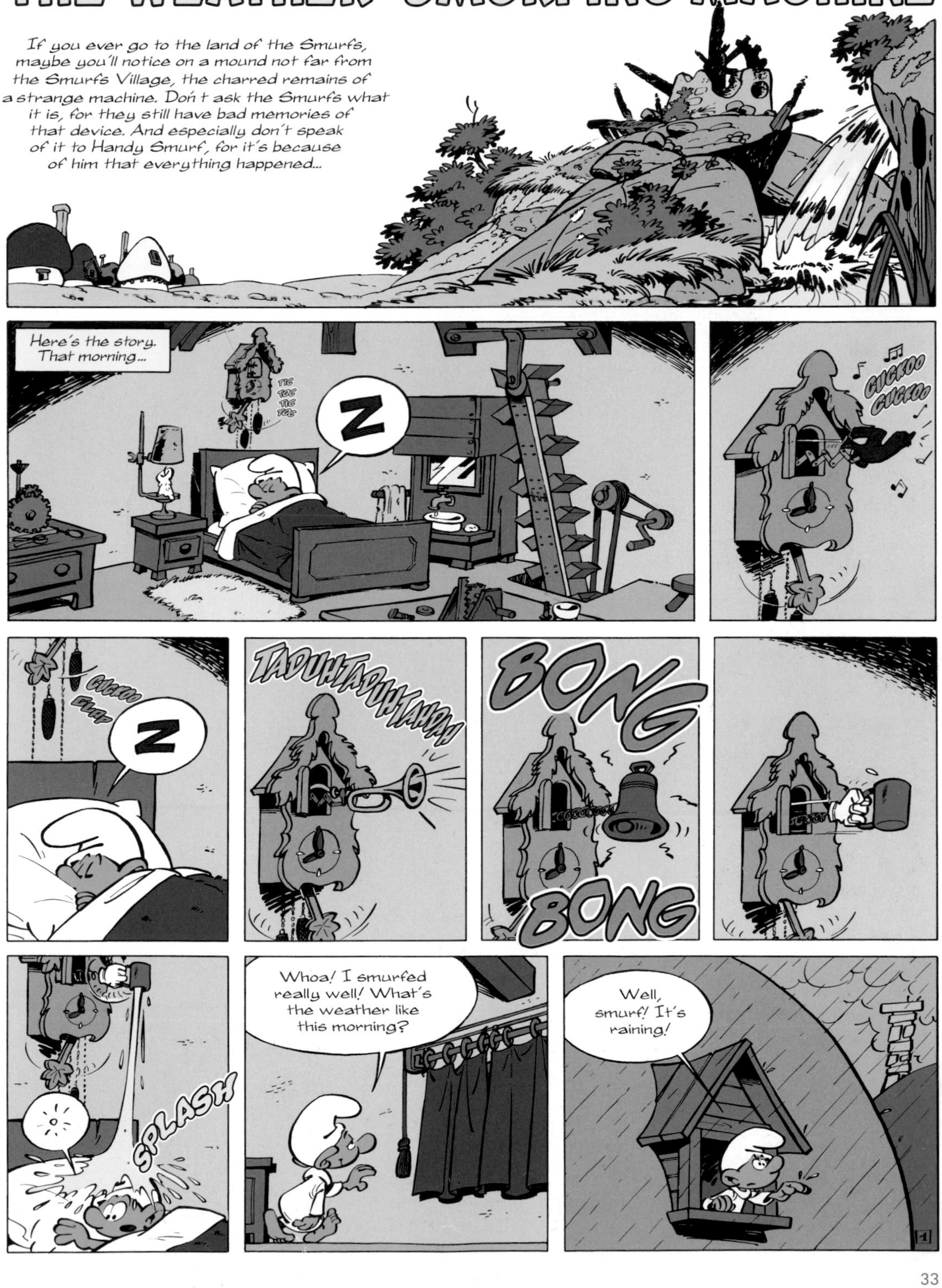
If you ever go to the land of the Smurfs, maybe you'll notice on a mound not far from the Smurfs Village, the charred remains of a strange machine. Don't ask the Smurfs what it is, for they still have bad memories of that device. And especially don't speak of it to Handy Smurf, for it's because of him that everything happened...
Here's the story. That morning...
Z
CUCKOO CUCKOO
CUCKOO
Z
BONG
BONG
SPLASH
Whoa! I smurfed really well! What's the weather like this morning?
Well, smurf! It's raining!
1

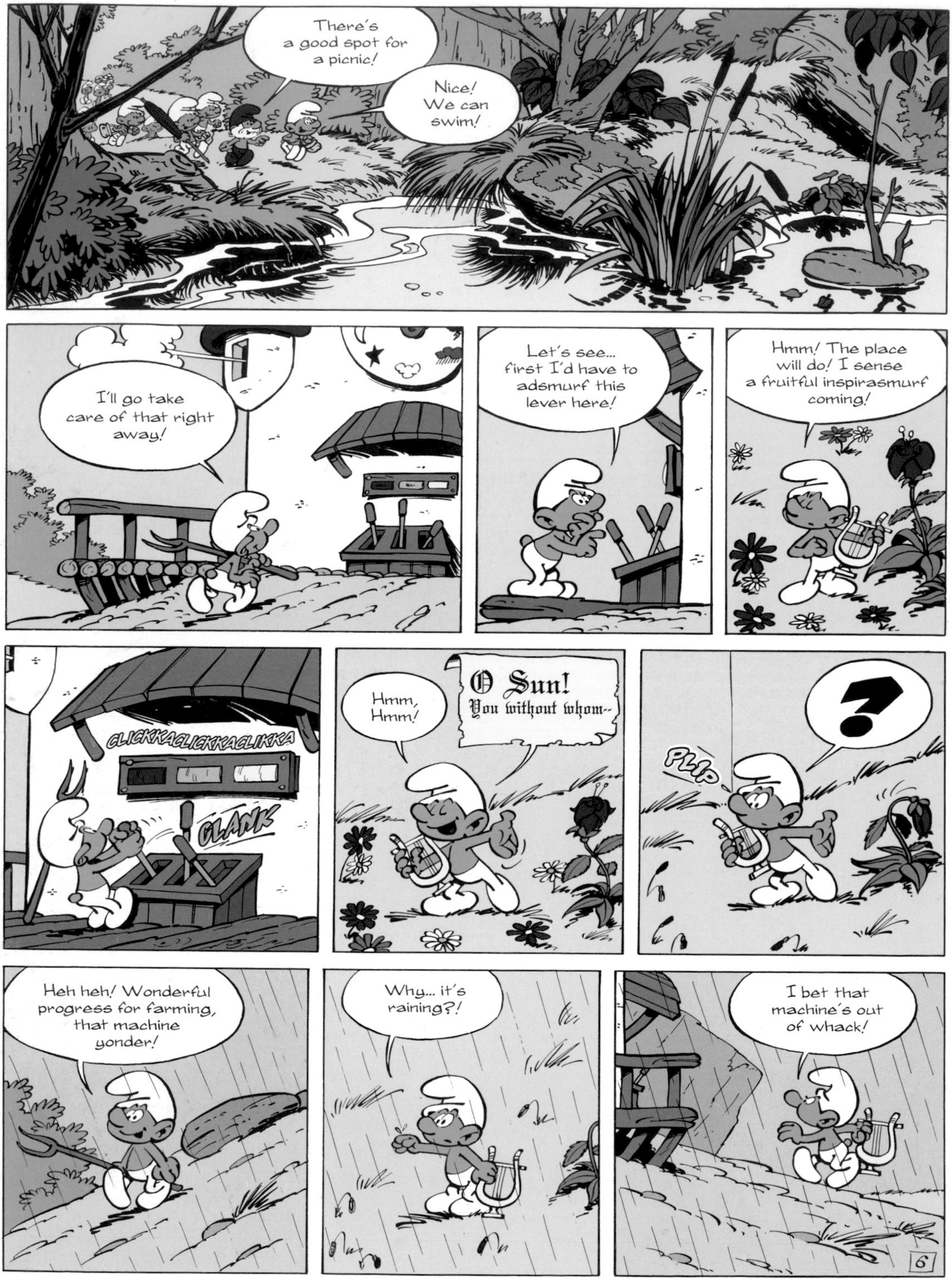
There's a good spot for a picnic!
Nice! We can swim!
I'll go take care of that right away!
Let's see... first I'd have to adsmurf this lever here!
Hmm! The place will do! I sense a fruitful inspirasmurf coming!
CLICKKACLICKKACLIKKA
CLANK
Hmm, Hmm!
O Sun! You without whom--
PLIP
?
Heh heh! Wonderful progress for farming, that machine yonder!
Why... it's raining?!
I bet that machine's out of whack!
6

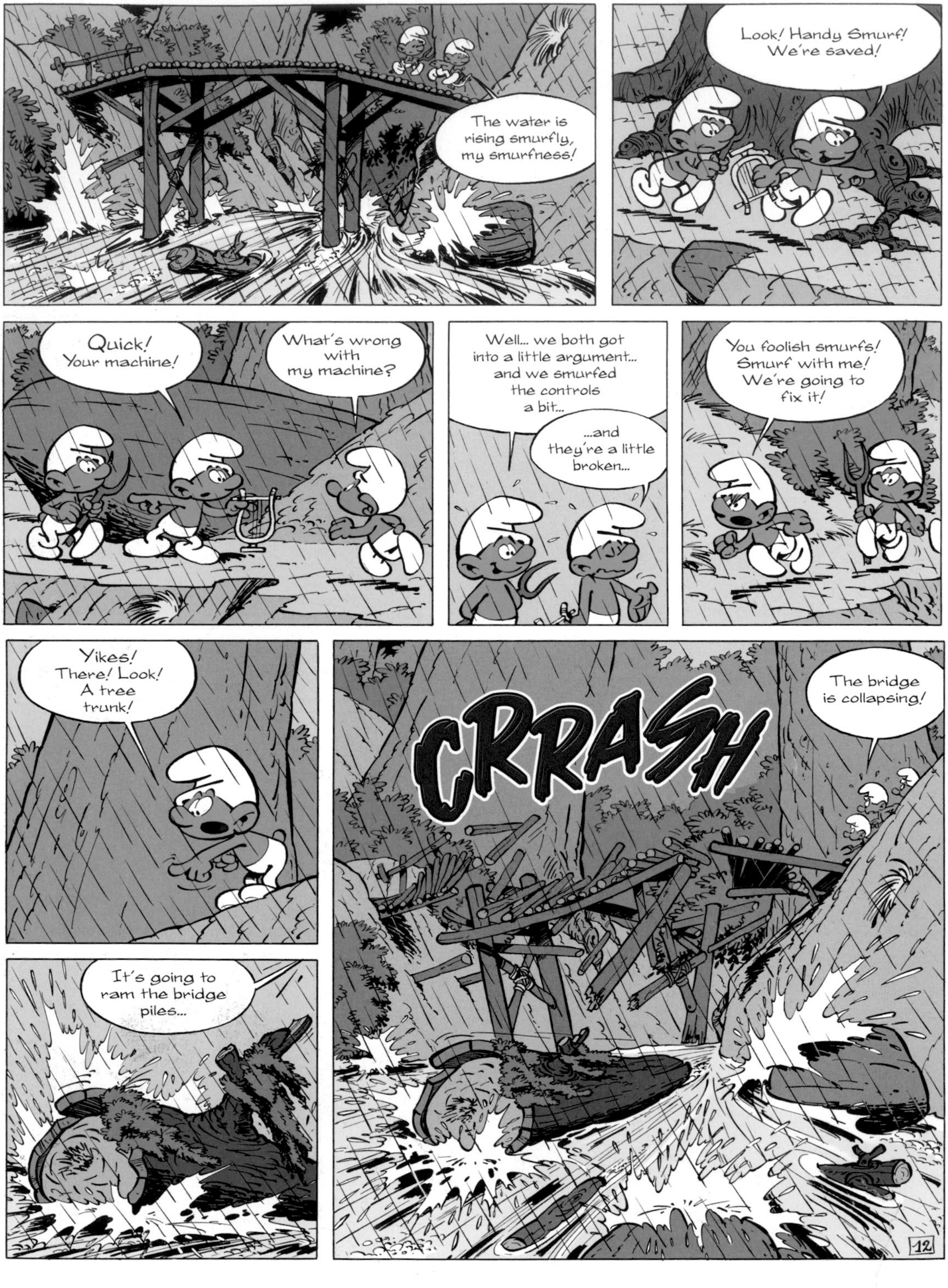
The water is rising smurfly, my smurfness!
Look! Handy Smurf! We're saved!
Quick! Your machine!
What's wrong with my machine?
Well... we both got into a little argument... and we smurfed the controls a bit...
...and they're a little broken...
You foolish smurfs! Smurf with me! We're going to fix it!
Yikes! There! Look! A tree trunk!
It's going to ram the bridge piles...
CRRASH
The bridge is collapsing!
12

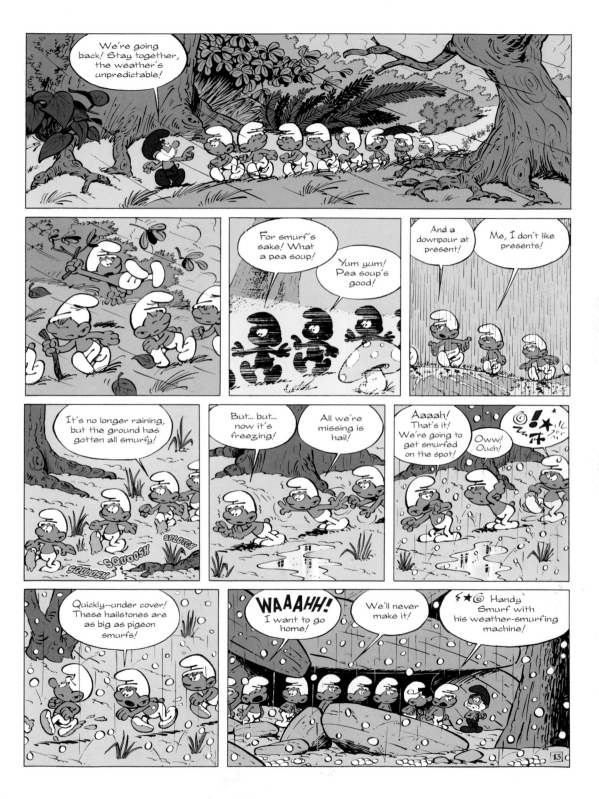

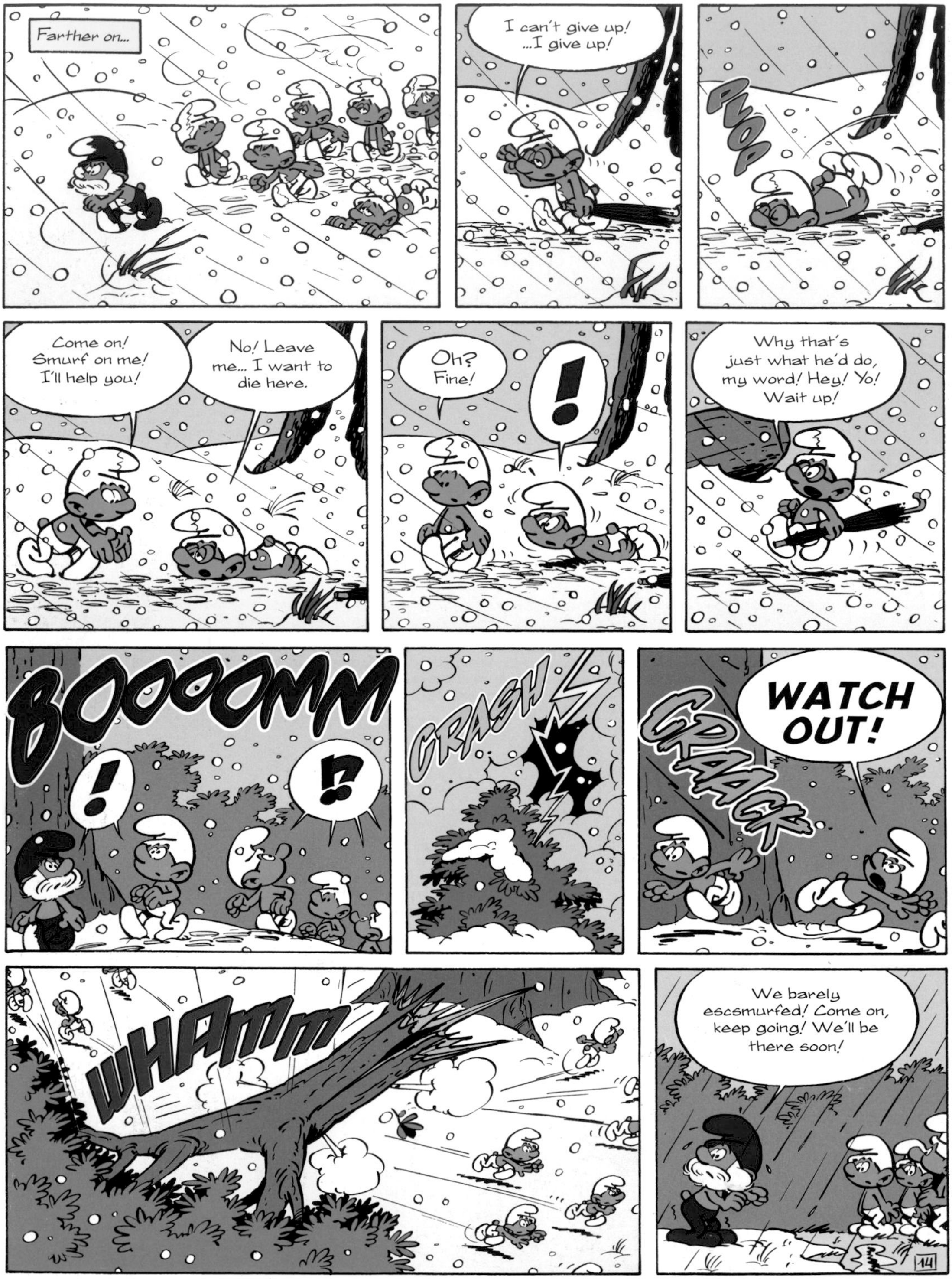

Farther on...
I can't give up! ...I give up!
PLOP
Come on! Smurf on me! I'll help you!
No! Leave me... I want to die here.
Oh? Fine!
!
Why that's just what he'd do, my word! Hey! Yo! Wait up!
BOOOOMM
!
!?
CRASH
CRAACK
WATCH OUT!
WHAMM
We barely escsmurfed! Come on, keep going! We'll be there soon!
14

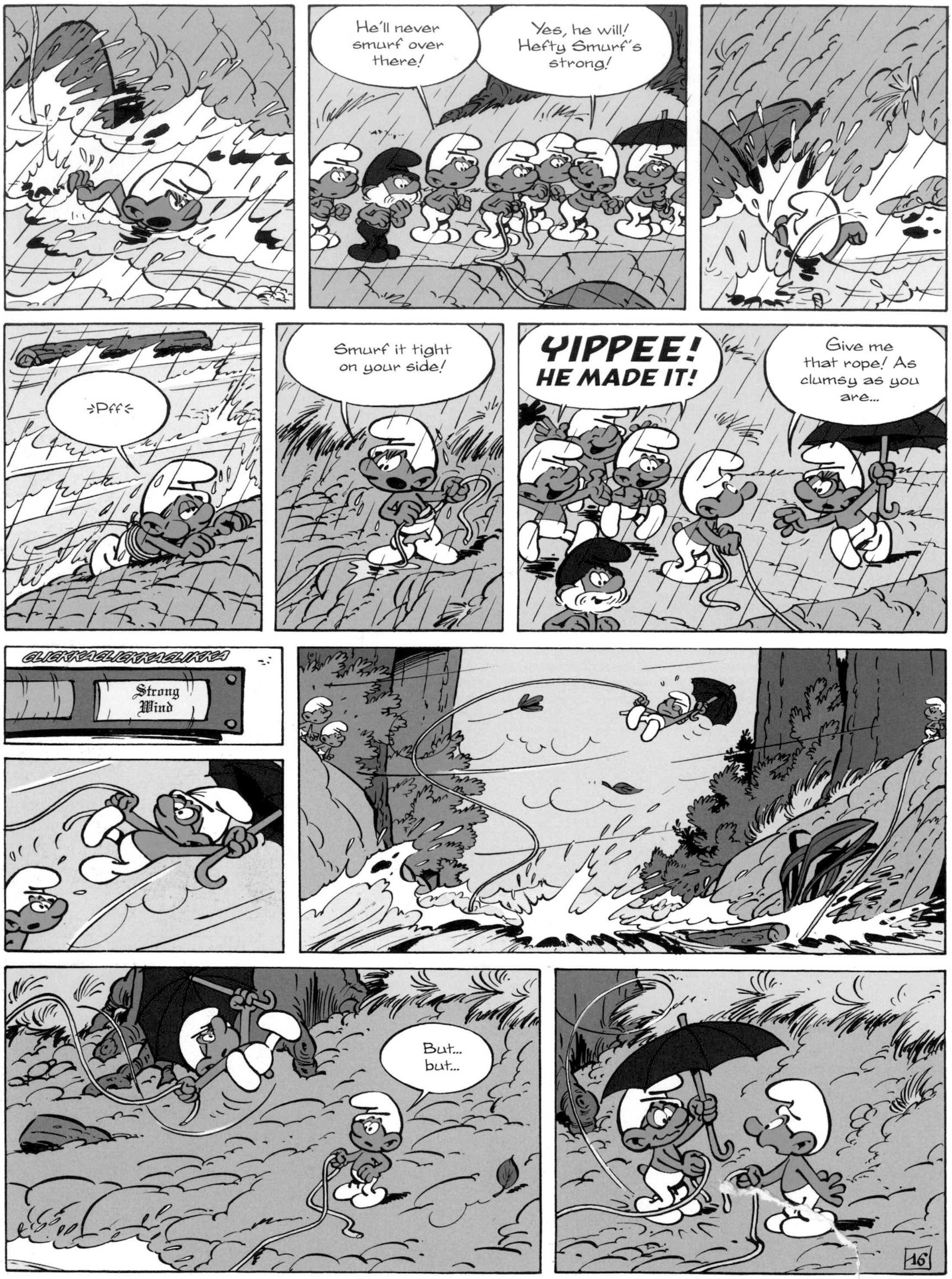
He'll never smurf over there!
Yes, he will! Hefty Smurf's strong!
≈Pff≈
Smurf it tight on your side!
YIPPEE! HE MADE IT!
Give me that rope! As clumsy as you are...
CLICKKACLICKKACLIKKA
Strong Wind
But... but...
16

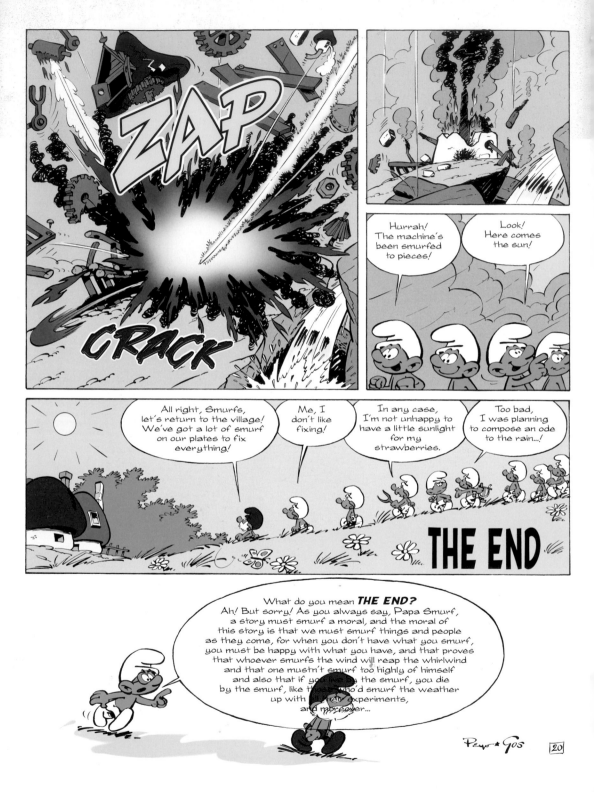

WATCH OUT FOR PAPERCUTZ

Welcome to the creatively fertile fourteenth SMURFS graphic novel by Peyo from Papercutz, the little company dedicated to publishing great graphic novels for all ages. I'm Jim Salicrup, the Smurf-in-Chief that refuses to change diapers.

Wow! You'd think that an event as exciting as the birth of a new Smurf would be THE major Smurf event of any year, and ordinarily, you'd be right. But, this year, there are so many exciting events happening, it may just make your head Smurf!

The biggest news is that Smurfs 2 will be opening soon at a theater near you on August 3, 2013. That's right, the sequel to the first smash Smurfs movie is coming out this year, featuring all the stars you loved from the first film in an all-new sequel set in France!

But that's not all! To celebrate the release of the new film, Papercutz has a couple of exciting projects also coming your way. We'll just tell you about one of them now, and announce the other in SMURFS #15. After all, we realize there's only so much Smurf-excitement a mere human can possibly handle.

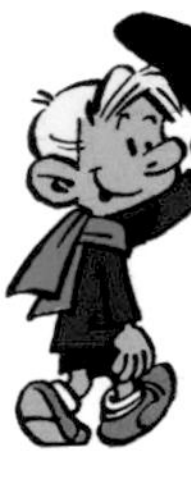

So, are you ready? Papercutz is proud to announce we will be publishing a new graphic novel series from Peyo, the creator of THE SMURFS, called BENNY BREAKIRON. It's about a young French boy with super-powers. "When I came up with Benny, I soon decided to give him an Achilles heel: when he gets a cold he loses all his strength," explained Peyo about his pint-size powerhouse. A far-too-brief sample of BENNY BREAKIRON, appears on the following pages, and BENNY BREAKIRON #1 "The Red Taxis" will be available soon at booksellers everywhere.

A Smurf Baby, a Smurf sequel, and a new Papercutz graphic novel series by Peyo—how exciting is that? If all that wasn't enough Smurfiness for you, then whatever you do, wherever you go, don't miss THE SMURFS #15 "The Smurflings," for the story that introduces even more young Smurfs, as well as another big SMURFS announcement!

Smurf you later!

Jim

THE RED TAXIS

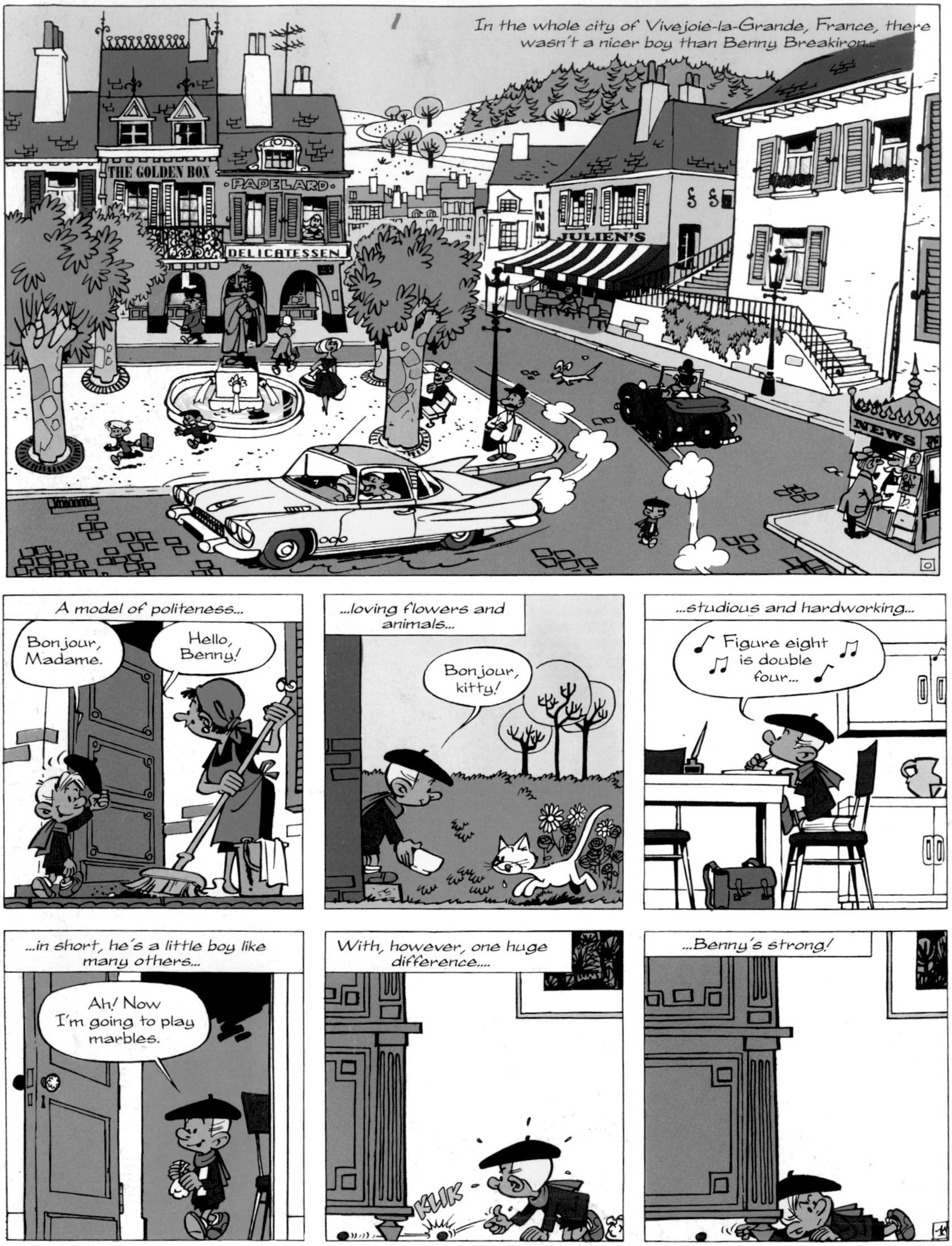

In the whole city of Vivejoie-la-Grande, France, there wasn't a nicer boy than Benny Breakiron...
THE GOLDEN BOX
PAPELARD
DELICATESSEN
INN
JULIEN'S
NEWS
A model of politeness...
Bonjour, Madame.
Hello, Benny!
...loving flowers and animals...
Bonjour, kitty!
...studious and hardworking...
Figure eight is double four...
...in short, he's a little boy like many others...
Ah! Now I'm going to play marbles.
With, however, one huge difference....
KLIK
...Benny's strong!

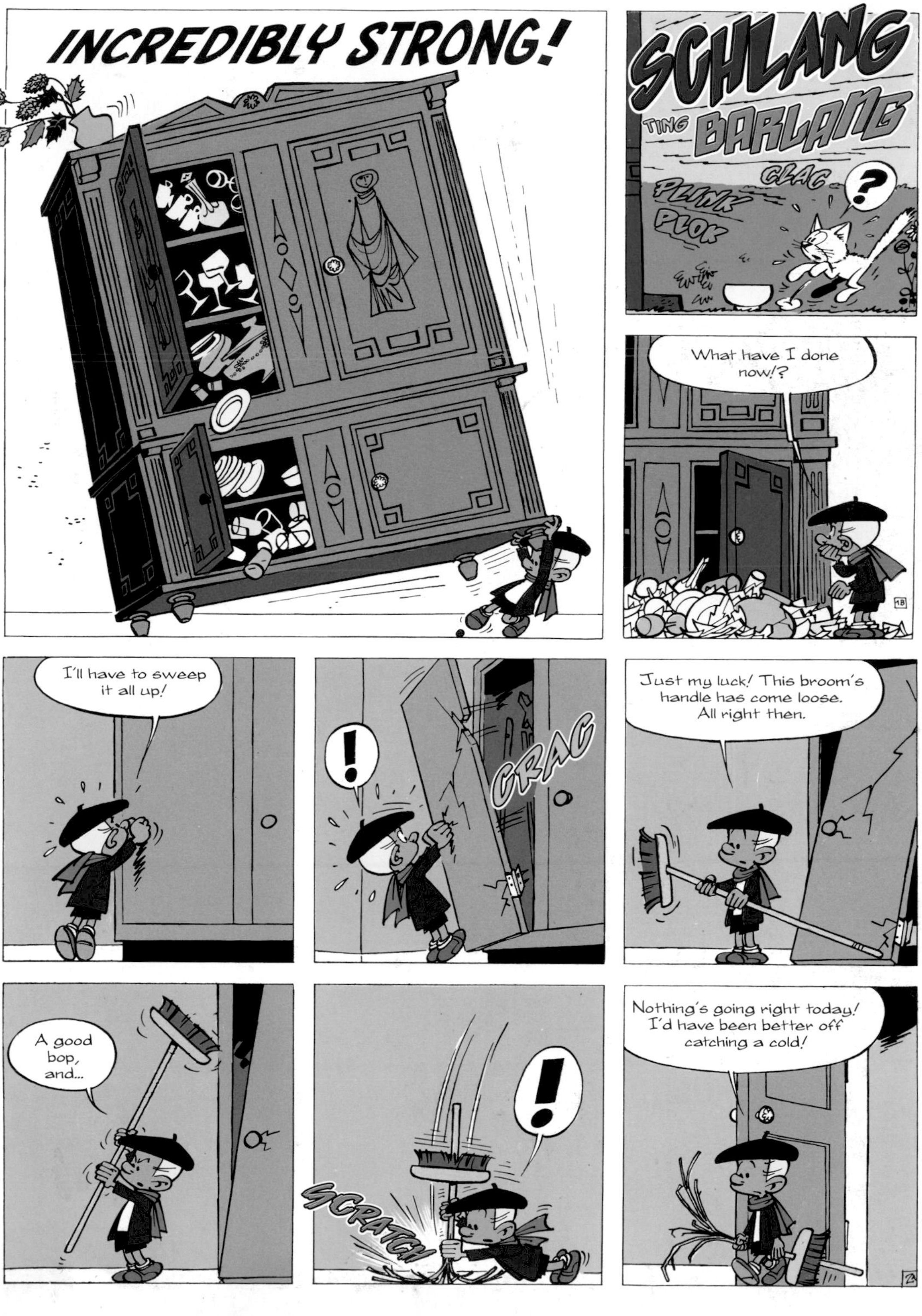
INCREDIBLY STRONG!
SCHLANG
TING
BARLANG
CLAC
PLINK
PLOK
?
What have I done now!?
I'll have to sweep it all up!
!
CRAC
Just my luck! This broom's handle has come loose. All right then.
A good bop, and...
!
SCRATCH
Nothing's going right today! I'd have been better off catching a cold!

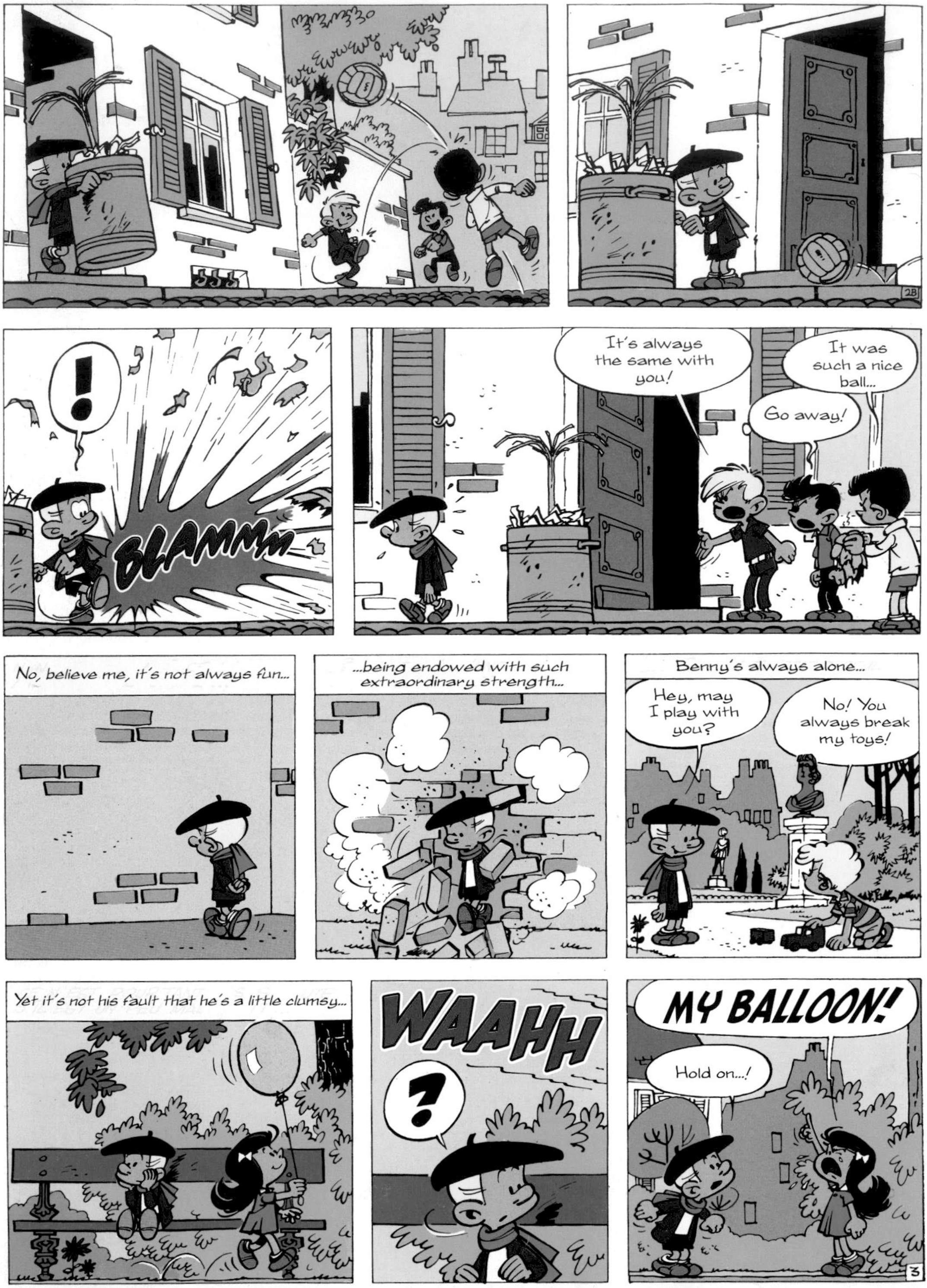

2B
!
BLAMMM
It's always the same with you!
It was such a nice ball...
Go away!
No, believe me, it's not always fun...
...being endowed with such extraordinary strength...
Benny's always alone...
Hey, may I play with you?
No! You always break my toys!
Yet it's not his fault that he's a little clumsy...
WAAHH
?
MY BALLOON!
Hold on...!
3

Will Benny be able to get the pink balloon back to the little girl? For the answer to that question, and much, much more—don't miss BENNY BREAKIRON #1 "The Red Taxis"—coming soon!

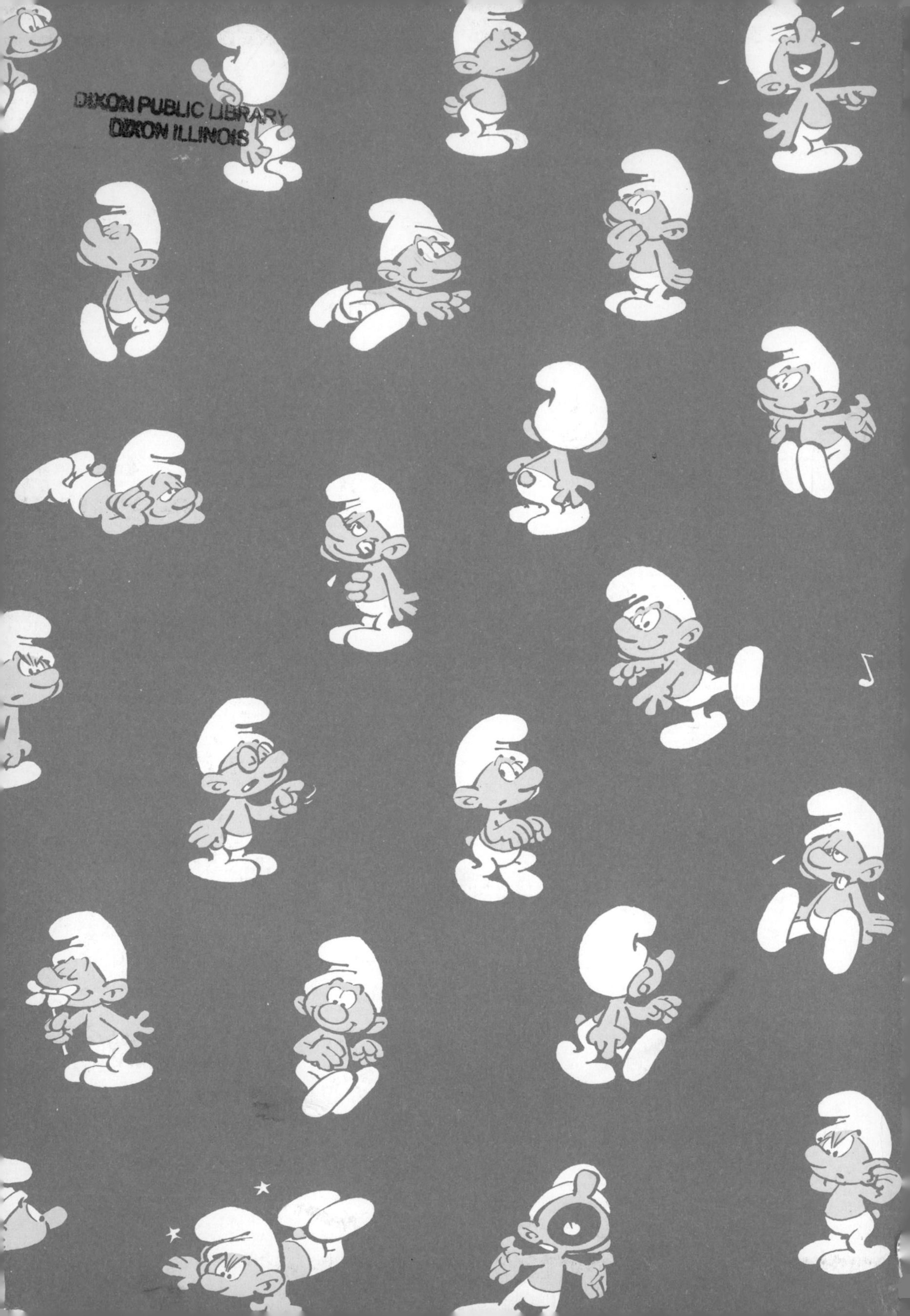